# PLUGS

## TATUM SAMSON

Tatum Samson

Library of Congress Control Number: 2018902853

ISBN: 1986007936
ISBN-13: 978-1986007931

Contact tatumsamson9@gmail.com with business inquiries.
tatumsamson.com

Tatum Samson

# DEDICATION

Dedicated to my parents,
for constantly supporting me,
and to you,
for giving the Plugs and me a chance.

# ACKNOWLEDGEMENTS

I can't believe the time has come to write my acknowledgements. I have been working on *Plugs* for three years, and to share this story means the world to me. I can see how much both my writing and I have changed since I began this journey. Without some people—who I will soon name—*Plugs* would not be the story it is today, and I would not be writing these acknowledgements.

I want to thank my parents, who support me unconditionally. When I tell them my dreams, they do not laugh or suggest something more realistic, but instead nod and ask, "How can we help you achieve them?" My parents have served as my fans, editors, and motivational speakers for the past three years. *Plugs* would not exist without them.

Thank you to my sister, for listening to my stories from the time I could speak.

I also want to extend a thank you to my eighth grade English teacher, Mr. Gagne, who not only facilitated my love for writing, but also provided valuable feedback on *Plugs* during its final stages.

Thank you to Ms. Garcia, Ms. Wren-Burgess, and Mr. Barrows for supporting my writing journey and always showing enthusiasm for my work.

Lastly, I would like to thank anyone who reads my book. I know that in today's busy world, sitting down and actually digesting a novel can be difficult. So, whether you read the first three pages or the entirety of the story, thank you for your dedication to the Plugs and me.

# PLUGS

# PROLOGUE
## BROOKLYN, NEW YORK, 1979 - P.E.I. HEADQUARTERS

A sharp ring distracted the Creator from his work as he shuffled the reports. Darting to the table, he flung his hand on the telephone and pressed the receiver against his ear.

A harsh, rugged voice whispered through the line. It sounded as fervent as he felt. "There's one in Boston. We're on our way to the hospital."

The sound of screeching tires overtook the voice, and the Creator slammed the phone back down. His adrenaline was pumping. This was it.

As the Creator raced to the headquarters' operating room, he heard the cries of a baby in the depths of the building. With every howl, he was reminded of another success, another discovery of a Plug. It was absolutely ingenious, and it all came down to physical science: piezoelectricity. If infants with heightened piezoelectric properties in their DNA could be found, then scientists could use the increased piezoelectric properties in their bodies to produce and harvest energy by applying pressure. He took pride in his creation, in his brilliant idea that was sure to fix the energy crisis shaking the country like an earthquake.

Over the years, Americans became accustomed to luxuries and comforts such as air conditioning, heating, stoves, and gas. These comforts that came with a developing economy had grown to a point where they were necessities, as important as breathing or eating, and with those necessities came the need for more energy. A never-ending cycle was formed; growth in standard of living required more energy which allowed for increased growth and so on. It would've turned out alright, if only the population was willing to live with the consequences of its greed and if the country could provide the resources itself. With power plants comes pollution; with wind turbines, tarnishing of the beauty of the landscape; with solar energy, high costs and unreliability. And with the need for oil, increased dependence on foreign countries. No one enjoyed the smells, sounds, or sights of what it took to fill their avarice. People felt passionate about keeping the environment safe, but still craved more and more energy. Citizens became demanding, deciding their wants were needs and their privileges were rights. But there was an issue—the issue of how to provide that energy. The oil supply had become a prominent focus of the government after the 1973 and 1979 energy crises. The United States didn't have the natural resources to supply the country's ever-increasing demand for energy, so it looked to the Middle East for a solution. Over time, the United States' dependence on the Middle East grew to frightening heights. The government grew desperate. So, a solution was found in the newly created Department of Energy; a solution so top secret, so controversial, that it needed to move completely underground. It would be called the Plugs Energy Initiative, or the P.E.I. for short.

Harvest the energy from humans; no smell, no noise, easy on the eyes, no compromises with other countries. Find six infants with a rare genetic mutation, one for each region of the United States. They would be the test subjects. Examine them, record findings, see if the living power plants worked. The government would run the experiment…it was an issue of national security. It would be top secret, confidential, unknown by all except for a small sector of the department. With the government's power, the experiment would have no limitations.

But it wasn't easy. There was a rare genetic feature required for one to be a Plug, an important trait that made the entire project of immeasurable value. Very few people contained the needed amount of shear stress in their DNA to power a growing population. Six children with this genetic trait needed to be found. And the lives of these children would be difficult. Five were already secured in the facility…only one more was required to make the experiment complete. That is what the agents in Boston had found: the final Plug.

***

A man in a black trench coat and newly shined shoes entered the hospital through a side door. Pulling out his walkie-talkie, he clicked onto channel nine.

"I'm here. Meet me by southeast door," he whispered into the device.

He slid the walkie-talkie back into his pocket and crouched beside the wall. He looked down at the baby in his arms and met eyes with the little girl wrapped in pink.

Her mouth popped open in surprise, and she started to cry.

The head doctor opened the door, a baby in his arms as well. He peered over his shoulder, shifted the lock into place, and hurried over to the man.

"Baby girl, seven pounds, three ounces. Her parents have only seen her once," the doctor reassured him.

"A perfect match. What were they going to name her?"

"Perri, I think. Perri Gering."

The two men held out the babies, switching them.

Perri slept through the movement.

The doctor sighed. "I'll need Perri's ID wristband."

The man in the trench coat slipped a tiny band off of Perri's wrist and dropped it into the doctor's palm.

Standing up, the doctor shook hands with the man. "Well, best of luck to you. Keep me updated."

The man nodded and watched as the doctor left the room with the new baby. He peered down at the tiny girl. Her eyelashes fluttered, and her cheeks were a flushed pink. "You are no longer Perri Gering…I think we'll call you…Emily."

And that was the last time Perri Gering's true name was spoken.

# CHAPTER ONE
## BROOKLYN, NEW YORK, P.E.I. HEADQUARTERS

They grew up in the headquarters; in a facility with adults in white coats who had brisk paces and long faces. The adults there never smiled, but they never frowned either, just kept their thin lips in a straight line and did as they were told. It wasn't a children's type of place to live; metal rooms lined the brightly lit hallways, Christmas was a foreign holiday, and every room was a dull shade of gray. The Plugs passed a long twelve years there; ate what they were told, did what they were told, transmitted energy. They never took a break; always working, always moving, always creating. They often found themselves tired beyond belief, barely able to stay on their feet when the sun went down, but it was all they were used to: work, eat, sleep, repeat. It was all they were made for, as they had been told.

But they had each other. The six Plugs, the only ones who knew what it felt like to live a life that wasn't theirs to live. Antonia, Emily, Troy, Lydia, Brice, and Jared. They grew up together, in their own way, doing whatever they could to make the best of the worst. Sure, it wasn't ideal, but they found family in one another, in these children only alike in one DNA trait and a difficult situation. As the Plugs ran on the treadmills, they dreamed about what their parents might be like. They played tag in the long and winding hallways and stayed up late in their bunk beds, whispering about the scientists, making jokes about the weirdest ones—the Plugs swore that a few of the scientists were aliens. Twelve years together, and no matter how terrible it became, no matter how long or tough each day, they all had someone to talk to when the night arrived. And life was okay.

# CHAPTER TWO
## 1991

It wasn't until the twelfth year of living at the facility that they were separated.

The scientists were confident with the experiment, satisfied with the energy the Plugs were producing. As a result, they moved them to different regions of the country; one Plug for each region. That was the plan.

Jared went to a facility in California. Antonia went to the lonely building in Albany. Troy was sent to North Carolina, Lydia to sweltering Arizona, Brice to Rhode Island, and Emily to Minnesota. The next phase of the experiment began, to determine if six people alone could supply energy for the six regions of the United States. To the scientists, it was an experiment, but to the Plugs, it was their life. It was hard to say goodbye, impossible to leave one another and all they knew. The lone anchor, the one sliver of sun peeking out of the gloomy clouds, was being pulled out from beneath them. There were tears and pleas to the scientists, the Plugs desperately begging to stay together. The pleas were ignored.

But before they were separated, the children promised each other one thing; one thing that would keep them courageous for so many years: that when they turned seventeen, they would meet in Kansas, the center of the country, and reunite. After their assigned birthday on April 1st, they would wait for each other at the Topeka Great Overland Station. One of the kinder scientists had grown up in Topeka, and in her bouts of guilt she would quietly tell them stories about where her family would visit when they lived in the city. She had loved trains as a child and dreamed of becoming a conductor, so every Saturday night, she'd go on long walks to the station with her family. The scientist would describe the most memorable details of the station that she had adored as a kid. The children's favorite story involved her brother clumsily climbing a red and blue structure in front of the building and shouting at the top of his lungs, "I'M ON TOP OF THE WORLD!"

To the Plugs' delight, some of the other scientists felt guilty as well, and this proved to be their view to the outside world. Although the stories of such grand adventures made them jealous, they loved to hear the tales that seemed almost fantastical. And these tales only increased their desire to be free. So, the Plugs would escape, and they would find each other, no matter the risk or danger or pain. And they knew it might be foolish to run away, knew it might only make their lives more difficult. But the promise remained. And life was bad until the time came to run.

# CHAPTER THREE
## Brooklyn, New York, 1991 - P.E.I. Headquarters

"Tape it over the camera, Troy! Hurry up!" Lydia's face peeked out from behind the crack in the door.

"I'm trying…ummm…Brice, is this right?" Jumping down from the black chair, Troy beckoned for Brice to check his handiwork.

"Oh, don't ask stupid, clumsy old Jared." Jared pouted in the corner. He looked like he'd smelled sour milk.

"Shut up! It doesn't matter, just get it done." The door opened an inch wider. Examining the security camera, Lydia smirked and threw open the door. "Good enough."

Emily stumbled in behind her. She was wringing her hands. With a light tap, she gained Lydia's attention. "You shouldn't talk so loudly. The security cameras can hear us!"

"No, they can't, Emily. Remember? I fixed that yesterday. And…" Antonia couldn't help herself. "They don't hear us, they record us and play it back." She was crossing her arms now.

Nodding, Emily drifted over to the carpet in the center of the floor and folded her legs gracefully.

Everyone joined her in a circle. Only Lydia seemed able to speak.

"Okay, so we're being separated tomorrow. We know that because they told us. And…we also know that we're each going to a different region, because you checked the database, right Antonia?"

"Right. At least, that's what their notes said." Antonia pulled out a sheet of paper covered in her thin writing. "I didn't have time to see who was going where, exactly." Regret filled her voice.

"It's fine, you did great." Emily placed her hand on Antonia's shoulder with a small smile.

"We don't have time for that," Brice huffed. Pulling a magazine out from under his bed, he flipped to page three. He'd been given the magazine by one of the more remorseful scientists…one of the scientists who had realized what he'd gotten into much too late. Scratchy circles identified each region in pen.

"There." Troy pointed to the center of the map. "Topeka. That's where Dr. Weine grew up." He let his finger rest on the city marking, drinking in the idea…the possible future.

"Yeah. Topeka, Kansas, here we come." Jared rubbed his hands together. His eyes twinkled.

"Okay, to clarify…" Lydia held up her hands, silencing the others. "When we turn seventeen, we'll meet up in Topeka, Kansas. Right under the figure at the Great Overland Station that Dr. Weine told us about. Get out however you can, and, above all else, keep our location secret. Got it?"

Silent, solemn nods all around the circle.

"I don't want to say goodbye to you guys," Antonia whimpered. "What if this doesn't work? What if we never, ever see each other again?"

"It'll work," Troy promised. "It'll work."

"How can you be so sure?"

"I just know. The good guys always win. That's how it's supposed to be."

"We're gonna make it. If not when we're seventeen, then when we're thirty, or sixty." Lydia's fists clenched and unclenched rapidly.

A clock chimed twice down the hallway.

"Happy birthday," whispered Jared.

Emily only grimaced. "Happy as can be."

# CHAPTER FOUR -- MITCH
## DULUTH, MINNESOTA, 1996

"Get up. Decision today."

"What decision, exactly?" Mitch mumbled as he rolled out of bed. A strand of tousled blonde hair fell over his right eye, and he blew it upwards, returning his mother's angry glare. Moments later, a loud yawn escaped his throat, which was greeted by an exasperated look from the tense woman.

Shaking her head, she folded her arms tightly and narrowed her eyes at the boy. They were an icy blue, and they seemed to chill whomever they fell upon. Mitch's mother heaved a sigh. She retrieved a tidily folded lab coat and tan khakis and placed them on the foot of his bed. She seemed to need a minute to gather her thoughts, but finally looked over at him calmly and began to speak.

"You're hopeless, Mitch. You'll be observing an experiment today, tested on the clarity and depth of your analysis, and if you're deemed qualified, you will be offered a job as a lab assistant in the Plugs project. Mitch, I'd like to warn you, if you say no, you still can't leave this place." Unfolding her arms, she widened her eyes at her son and turned away, pacing around the room.

Blinking to clear the fogginess out of his eyes, Mitch sat up and looked over at his mother. "I know I'm pretty much stuck in this place. Thanks for that, by the way," he responded.

It wasn't an unusual thing, for the two to have a rather unpleasant interaction that mainly consisted of sarcasm—that is, if they had any interaction at all. His mother was constantly working, and it was clear to him that when it came to their relationship, she enjoyed pretending it simply didn't exist.

He and his mother had never developed a good understanding of one another, never bonded. Secrets about her job and her constant prioritizing of work ripped apart the seams of their thin connection until everything had become too unraveled to stitch back together. Anyways, he had been a mistake, and his mother told him that multiple times. When her husband left without notice because of her job, she seemed to harden, and her expectations of all people sank to nonexistent. Mitch couldn't help but notice that after his father left, Linda focused even more on her work. He thought she must be trying to prove that the project was worth all she had lost. What hurt the most was that all Mitch had done with his life so far was sit cooped up in his room, not a Plug and not a scientist; so, in his mother's eyes, nothing.

"See you in the test room in ten minutes. Don't embarrass me, Mitch. This is your only future. If you don't understand piezoelectricity by now, you never will. It's not that confusing, not if you actually choose to listen. Apply pressure to a piezoelectric force and squeeze the atoms to produce mechanical energy. Convert that energy to electricity." She clapped her hands on each word. With that, she left the room, slamming the door behind her and muttering.

Dressing quickly, Mitch managed to knock over his bedside lamp and sent glass flying across the hard wooden floors. Refusing to clean it up, he brushed the shards under his bed. The bit of sunlight coming through the window shone against the wood, but most of it was blocked by his hefty dresser. He had always wondered why he would need a dresser so big if he only owned a few items. Changing his mind, he knelt to the floor and began to gather up the glass shards from under the bed, sweeping them into a towel and depositing them into his trash can where they made a hollow *ting!* He knew his mother would hate him even more for keeping his room a mess. At this point, he would try anything to make her like him even the tiniest bit.

When he reached the experiment room minutes later, he shielded his eyes from the blinding brightness. Fluorescent bulbs sent spots swimming through his vision. Mitch gaped at the scene. The space was mainly filled with a two-way mirror, where the scientists could see through to the Plug named Emily, but she couldn't see them. A plate of food sat in a corner, as if this was some social event, not an observation. Mitch peered across the room, studying the control panels that made up the right wall. Lights blinked in correspondence with the display's letter keys, all the way to the very edge of the wall, where they met with the mirror. Mitch's gaze traveled to the girl. In the room on the other side of the mirror, Emily lie strapped to a metal table shivering.

Mitch recalled all that he knew: Emily had more piezoelectricity in her DNA than anyone else, and she supplied energy for one region of the country. Other than that, he was a stranger to the actions of the facility. Sometimes he avoided the questions he had about Emily's life at all costs. And today, he was glad to be so unaware.

He had mainly expected her to sit down to a written test, maybe see how long it took to run a mile. Something easy, something she wouldn't mind. But this was different: she seemed upset, scared. She was his age, only sixteen, almost seventeen, and the fear was obviously visible on her face...between her creased brows, in her clenched jaw.

"Hey, what're you doing?" he whispered to the scientist standing near the control panels, holding a clipboard and aligning wires with outputs. Mitch knew he shouldn't talk so casually, but the sight of the girl made him nervous. The way she tightened her fists and squeezed her eyes shut sent a shaky jolt through his body.

A man in the connected room inserted six wires on either side of Emily's waist, arms, and legs. Realization passed over the girl's face, and she began shouting. Her eyes popped open like the roller on a window shade being snapped up.

The man who had placed the wires exited the room, completely ignoring her.

Mitch was beginning to feel more uneasy, afraid for the girl. She obviously wasn't willing to do this, didn't want to be here. Suddenly, a buzzing sound filled the room, electricity flying through the wires. Instantaneously, they reached the girl. She shrieked and desperately tried to free herself from the metal clamps around her wrists. Emily's body fought against the restraints, but her limbs flailed uselessly.

"Interesting…the stress caused by electrocution provides three times the energy produced by addition of one third body weight to the subject" muttered Mitch's mother, acting as if she were chatting about the weather. She scratched away on her clipboard, murmuring to herself. Mitch thought he saw the hint of a smile on her lips.

Another screech echoed through the room as Emily ran her fingers along the cold torture bed. She continued to shriek louder. Her screams scratched Mitch's throat, sending rocketing pulses through his heart.

"Get her out of there!" Mitch shouted at the top of his lungs, running to his mother and tugging on her arm. "You're hurting her! What are you doing?" His questions were only interrupted by Emily's howls, still bouncing off of the white walls.

His mother shooed him away, shaking her head and continuing to watch the girl struggle. "You must prove yourself. Forget emotion and focus on the science. It is all you can rely on here. I thought you knew that," she hissed.

"Let her out!" he hollered, banging against the glass. The sight of her writhing figure was unbearable. He was ripped from the mirror and thrown to the floor. Crawling to the control panel, flicking the switch, and pulling out the wires he had seen the man connect were the last things he did before the world went black in his eyes.

# CHAPTER FIVE -- EMILY
## DULUTH, MINNESOTA, 1996

The wind howled outside the facility, waking Emily up with a start. The sudden movement sent her caramel hair flying. It sounded like an animal was trying to claw its way into her bedroom, desperate for safety from the raging storm. She glanced around, but finally settled down once she'd made sure no one was lurking in the dark corners of her room.

Her room was as lifeless as ever. The empty floor, spotless rug, and off-balance night stand stood as they had when she'd fallen asleep, casting the same shadows across the floor as before. Rain splattered against the meager window. There weren't many windows in the Minnesota facility, and Emily noticed this a long time ago, when she first arrived in her new home. For a while she had wondered why, and now she knew that it was because the scientists didn't want the outside world tempting her. They constantly warned her of what would occur if she left the safe confines of the building; promises of pain and cruelty much worse than that which she was already subjected to. But life outside of the facility never seemed to stop calling Emily's name.

Lying on her back, staring up at the ceiling, Emily wished she were looking at the shining stars, not at the bare white walls and the newly dusted vent that sent warm air whooshing through the room. She wished she were lying in the grass, not in a hard bed. Next to her, she wished she had someone to keep her company during the storm, not a sterile night stand.

In the loud wind, a million thoughts ran through her head all at once in a jumble of memories. She remembered the promise she and her friends had made years ago. It felt like a lifetime of waiting, but it would only be a day now until she'd try to escape and see them for the first time in so long. Until then, she had work to do. Most importantly, she must conceal her plans of escaping from the closely watching guards and scientists who examined her every move.

An eternity passed with her just lying there, silent, breathing in and out, trying to calm her energized nerves. She could feel her hands twitching by her sides, her toes cold with the thought of rebelling against everything she'd been taught. But it also sent a warm sensation through her chest, a satisfaction at the mere thought.

Her ears searched through the rainfall, sifting through it like sand, waiting for something to break through the noise besides the hums and creaks of machines. She lay alone, listening to the storm envelop her. Finally, her daze was interrupted by a knock on the door. Before Emily could utter "come in" the knob turned and the door was thrust open. She'd almost forgotten in her trance: there was no privacy here.

It was only Linda, the bony faced, rigid woman who set Emily's schedules and directed her every move, every task, every day. She had a tight face, and her hair was pulled into a bun so taut that her eyebrows always appeared a bit raised. Linda's lips opened only to speak of business, while her eyes opened only to seek the flaws of others. It seemed to Emily that Linda was very disconnected from the world, like nothing mattered but the thoughts running through her own mind. Emily almost felt bad for the woman…almost.

"What are you doing?" she snapped. "Get up! You're supposed to be running on the treadmill in five minutes."

"Sorry, just tired," Emily muttered, trying her best not to show that she had been up most of the night planning possible escape routes. There were only a few to sort through, but she had to be smart about it. If she were going to leave unnoticed, she'd need to use her wit and keen senses every bit to her advantage.

In three minutes, she was dressed in the standard sweatpants and tee shirt, and was subsequently whisked off to the gym, escorted by a rather miserable looking Linda. Not a word was uttered during their walk. Once they reached the double doors marking the entrance, Linda pushed one open, not bothering to hold it for Emily.

The gym was a large room with a tall ceiling, yet every inch of space was taken up by the equipment. It reminded Emily of the entire facility, of how the scientists tried to make it airy and comfortable, but squeezed so much into every space that there was no room to breathe. Treadmills lined the walls, only inches apart, and exercise equipment scattered the floor like an abandoned circus. The room had a disturbing air about it, as if someone was lurking in the corner to study each subject who entered. Outside, a gloomy, drizzling sky made Emily wonder if God himself was crying upon the world.

Surprisingly, a young boy with shaggy blonde hair was also running on a treadmill far across the room, peeking over his shoulder every few moments with a look of trepidation. His stare made Emily pause, but her curiosity battled with her discomfort and she peered towards the boy. Emily stepped onto the treadmill, aware of Linda's eyes following her. At first, the scientists had treated her like family, tried to make her feel at home. Now, she was nothing more than an overused lab rat; another pawn in the struggle to end the energy crisis. They had to keep her fit, fed, and rested. It was when she overheard Linda say "It needs sleep" one night that the harsh reality crashed down upon her: she wasn't made to be human. She was made to be a piece of machinery.

Once she began running, her feet slapping against the revolving treadmill cloth, Linda started to read off the tasks of the day.

"Eight AM, breakfast. Nine AM, you're hooked up to the sensors."

The rest of Linda's instructions were a blur to Emily, who was counting down the moments until she would leave. Emily breathed a sigh of relief and ran through her mind everything she had to do today, searching for slots of time to finalize an escape plan in her head and come to terms with her fear. She was tired of the forced exercise, the sensors, the harvesting of electricity. So, Emily continued to run until all she could hear was her own breathing, a sort of pattern that seemed to be the only thing she could control at the moment. She dreamed of a day where she could control more than that. She dreamed of flying far away from this place until it was only a distant memory, miles behind her. Emily upped the speed and ran.

She wondered about her friends, if their time had been as lonely as hers, if their scientists were as strict and disturbing. She wondered how tall they would be, how much they had changed; if they'd grown tougher, if they'd grown softer. No matter what, Emily was just glad to see the familiar face of a friend. A sharp pang stabbed at her chest. It was worse that she actually remembered them; it made her fully understand how much had been taken from her at such a young age.

She was starting to grow tired, her breaths becoming less of a pattern and more like short gasps that interrupted her steady stream of thought. The treadmill seemed too quick now, much quicker than it had when she first started, but Linda had ordered her to run for an hour. She had to do an hour. Linda would come and check the time, and if it was only forty-five minutes, she'd make her do double tomorrow. Emily was sick of being a slave. Sick of following every order and command. Emily needed this, just this one tiny act of defiance. She was done being a puppet. But she couldn't bring herself to do it. Fear took over her decisions again and again.

So she ran.

When Linda came to check on her, she seemed slightly disappointed, as if she hoped Emily would make a mistake so that she could yell at her. While she searched the treadmill to find the speed, writing down notes in her log, Emily checked her agenda, where her schedule was neatly scrawled across the paper in symmetrical boxes. Next, she had breakfast. They always made her run before breakfast. The scientists believed it would be motivation to keep going. Emily disagreed. She thought it only made her dizzy, to run so long without having anything to eat. But she didn't have a say in the matter. She would just nod and go and move and repeat.

\*\*\*

The food they served was the same, bland type every day. Egg yolks and milk made for a mediocre breakfast, yogurt and fruit for a subpar lunch, and walnuts with chicken for a slightly better dinner. Emily felt a strange empathy for the cafeteria workers. Sadness always boiled up in her chest when she saw them, catching a glimpse of how unenthusiastic about life they were. The workers never had an expression on their face, just a mask of indifference. The egg yolks were dumped onto her plate by an old man, where they bounced once and finally came to a rolling stop. Then she was immediately ushered to her seat alone.

Every day, Emily sat in the same seat, Linda recording the amount of protein she consumed. Linda then would send the data to the nutritionist. But this time, Emily wasn't chickening out. Even the littlest change, the littlest act of defiance, felt like a war had been won. So, when Linda pointed to her seat, she turned and walked to her room, instead. It felt amazing.

She could hear Linda following her, probably to question why she would dare to think for herself after so many years of allowing her life to be completely controlled. But Emily reached her room before Linda could turn the hallway's corner, and she slammed the door. Surprising even herself, Emily jammed her desk chair under the door knob.

Linda banged on Emily's door for three minutes. Finally, she gave up and left, leaving Emily to map out some escape routes. She could try to fit through her window, but that was usually locked from the outside. She could also sneak through the cafeteria, but most of the time people were there to grab a late-night snack. The last route was the quickest, but the riskiest. It was straight down the hall, and then a quick right. Since all the bedrooms were in the same wing as her's, there was a chance someone might be up when she tried to execute her plan. Emily folded her paper into small squares and shoved it behind her night stand. She prayed Linda wouldn't find it. And then she prayed for her friends. Emily hoped they would make it out safe, too. But her prayers were stopped by Linda, who's screechy voice seeped through the door. "Sorry to interrupt your little meditation, but you've got to go prepare for your appointment. Now. It will take a few hours, and we want you to be up and working tomorrow," Linda said matter-of-factly.

Emily froze.

She had forgotten about the "cleaning." It was her least favorite part of living at the facility. Once a month, she required a test to clarify that she was "running smoothly." The scientists were constantly worried that her plug would suffer from metal fatigue or that she would suddenly malfunction. Anger exploded in Emily's chest, threatening to burst out of her. Why must they call it a cleaning, like she was some car that had grown too dirty for use; like she was some broken machine at the mercy of its creators? She couldn't control herself. In this moment, she didn't care if her actions meant that Linda would be suspicious of her. Emily needed confrontation. Swinging open the door, she stared straight into Linda's eyes.

"No."

# CHAPTER SIX -- TROY
## CHARLOTTE, NORTH CAROLINA

The sun was just peeking over the city skyline like a soft flame when Troy
woke up. Buildings and skyscrapers rose in the distance, the sunlight
glinting off of their metallic sides enough to make him want to shade his
eyes. Being stuck in the stuffy facility was made all the more tortuous with
the city so close by. He had never been able to see the tall buildings up
close, always on the other side of the pristine wall.

Rolling out of bed, Troy shuffled to the small window and sat on its
ledge, still big enough for him to fit. This was his favorite spot in the world
and had been since he was twelve. This was his escape: Troy's Place.
Although the metal was cold and the window was small, the discomfort
was well worth the glimpse. He did this everyday, to remind himself that
there was a world outside; that there was more to see than stark white
hallways with bright fluorescent lights. Sometimes he thought that he'd
have gone insane without the window; just an empty shell, a body with a
melting mind. No matter how much the scientists tried to convince him
that the facilities were top-notch, that they had everything anyone could
ever want, he didn't believe them, not one bit. Troy pressed his nose up
against the glass and squinted. Before he was completely against the
window, he could see his eyes in the reflection, staring back at him as if

they belonged to someone else, someone standing on the other side. They were a cold, frosty blue, and he was always surprised with how lost they looked. Those two eyes seemed to capture all the pain of being locked away like an animal.

He decided that this window was his best chance of escape, despite the small size. Most of the scientists in the facility trusted Troy, thought he was just a shy kid who would never disagree with them or speak up. But he'd been disagreeing with them for his entire life. Troy didn't think it was right to raise kids only to use them as machines. He didn't think it was right to give them no say in their own lives. But that's why he and his friends had decided to leave when they turned seventeen. Anger bubbled up inside him, but as always, he tried to push it back down and maintain his calm nature. He reminded himself to keep his composure.

One final sigh made the window too opaque to see through, and Troy reluctantly gave up to dress himself for the day.

A knock sounded on the door like a gunshot. It echoed around the empty space. Troy stood up slowly and turned the knob, peeking out a bit before swinging it fully open. It was only the old man, Mr. Miele, who had been assigned to monitor him. His white hair always stuck up in tufts around his little plump face. He seemed to be a happy person, his cheeks forever a bit red, like he had just sat through a wind storm. It was hard to be angry with a man like this, and Troy always tried to push aside his feelings of resentment for Mr. Miele. After all, he was only trying to help.

"Oh, Mr. Miele, hi," he said in surprise.

"Troy! Great boy, already up and runnin', good kid, good kid. Hey, it's a nice day, I tell ya, lots o' sun to soak up and enough hard-boiled eggs to see ya through the year, 'ey?" His mustache shook as he chuckled, making Troy almost smile to himself. He couldn't help but be amused by the man's fun spirit.

"Great, thanks…and good morning to you, too," Troy managed to sneak in between the man's hearty laughs, already on his way to the breakfast hall.

"Hey, wait up, son," he babbled.

Troy slowed his footsteps to please the man and peered over his shoulder, where he saw Mr. Miele awkwardly shuffling towards him. It was a confusing feeling, to like someone even if he trapped you in a life you never wanted.

Once he caught up, he started to breath heavily. A droplet of sweat collected around the edges of his forehead. Troy frowned, worrying that Mr. Miele might be sick. Despite his deep-rooted bitterness, Troy naturally felt concerned for the old man's health.

"Bad knee," Mr. Miele confessed, looking at the ceiling and scrunching up his eyes for a second, almost as if he were trying to squeeze the pain out of himself.

"Are you alright?" Troy questioned.

"Just fine, don't you worry. You've already got enough to think about with your appointment today, right?"

Troy winced at the mention of it, imagining the cold scientist who always completed the examination.

"Sorry, forgot ya didn't like to talk about it."

Troy could think of a thousand things he wanted to say, but he wasn't in the practice of offending the only person who actually talked to him.

"No worries," he gulped. He always tried his best to hide his feelings, especially from Mr. Miele. He wondered if the old man really liked him, or if it was all a well thought out act to guilt him into behaving. Either way, his mind was made up. He had to get out of the place, had to see the world and his friends. His heart was set on it, now more than ever before. He'd spent too much time in captivity, and every day drove him further from hope, deeper into the isolation of his mind.

The two of them turned the corner to the breakfast hall. The walls near the large doorways were home to a long window that looked out upon the grass behind the facility. The appearance of a window bigger than a shoebox was a gift to Troy, a glimpse to the city outside. Every day, he slowed by that window, constantly restraining himself from jumping through it and landing on the grass below, running as fast and as far away as he could. But for now, he needed to wait. Soon, he might just be free and much less lonely. If he tried to run away at the wrong time, he would be caught, extra security measures put up. He had to watch and wait for that perfect moment. Watch and wait…

*** 

Egg yolk was stuck in Mr. Miele's mustache as he chomped on his breakfast, a big plate of food sitting in front of him that was already half empty. Swallowing, he put down his fork long enough to to ask, "Hey, whatcha thinkin' in that head' o' yours?" He chuckled at himself and took a swig of water, some sloshing down onto his tee shirt.

When Troy turned from collecting his food in the cafeteria, he saw Mr. Miele watching him carefully, studying his every move. Troy began to worry that he was growing suspicious.

Was Mr. Miele really just making sure he didn't do anything out of the ordinary? Was the only friend he had…a phony?

"Earth. To. Troy," the old man jabbered, "Anyone there? Helloooo? Really, bud, what are you thinking about?" He leaned in a little, as if waiting to hear a secret. A click sounded. It had come from his pocket: a sleek black voice recorder. This man was no friend. He was a babysitter. Troy's fears were confirmed. Pushing himself away from the table, he returned to his only safe spot—his room—to wait for the dreaded examination that was to come. And although Troy didn't like to admit it, the revelation of why Mr. Miele spoke to him, why he showed any kindness at all, stung harshly.

Later that day, Troy waited in anticipation for his appointment. The examination room had a thick, humid feel to it, and shadows criss-crossed the walls, creating black splotches that hung like draped curtains. When Troy first walked in, he thought no one was there; the room was as if it had been deserted for years, not a whisper to pierce the air. But Troy had to remind himself that he had been in this very room only one month ago, and, taking a deep breath, he sat on the metal table, peering around him every few seconds. He tried to be brave, but this room always made his hands shake the slightest bit.

Suddenly, a screeching noise filled the entire space, nails on a chalkboard, magnified intensely. A chair squealed along the floor, obviously scratching the previously spotless tile. At the same time, a dark shape formed in the corner: a tall, gangly man. As the figure emerged from the shadows, Troy's breath hitched in his chest. It was the doctor who completed the examination of his plug every single month. But something was clearly wrong; something terrible.

# CHAPTER SEVEN -- LYDIA
## TUSCON, ARIZONA

Lydia was already up and eating in the cafeteria when Mrs. Tyren click-clacked up in her jet black, sky high heels. The woman's face looked much too old for her age, as if she had seen too much sorrow in her short time here and aged ten years in the time of one.

Grumbling a "What?" through her full mouth and taking a big gulp of soda, Lydia slammed the can back down onto the table as its contents splattered onto the already sticky surface.

"Lydia, you know you aren't supposed to drink soda, especially not this early! It'll drain your energy for the day and it's—"

"Don't you want me to be happy so that I'm more 'easily controllable?'" interrupted Lydia, making air quotes with her fingers. Putting as much innocence into her eyes as possible, she peered up at the wrinkled face of the young woman and blinked a few times. Lydia couldn't feel anything but hatred for these people. The only joy she gained in staying at the facility was making sarcastic comments towards those who had imprisoned her there for so long. But who could blame her?

"Well, I mean, yes…but…"

"Then let me drink my soda and wish I were anywhere but here in peace," quipped Lydia, throwing every bit of resentment she felt into the words and whipping back around to face her omelette.

"I'm going to pick up your schedule. I'll be back in two minutes, and I expect you to be done eating by then." Mrs. Tyren grimaced as she watched Lydia chug the rest of her soda. Finally, she turned to leave.

Lydia peered through the curtain of her hair to watch her trudge out of the room.

The second she was gone, Lydia was standing up and dumping the contents of her plate into the sink. She was leaving. Actually leaving. Tomorrow. Like, 24 hours from this very moment. The thought exhilarated Lydia, sent adrenaline coursing through her veins. Her friends. The only people who actually cared about her…the only people she actually cared about. She missed them more than she had thought possible. Their absence was a dull throb, like a toothache that never quite goes away. But the plan was made, everything in place.

There was one part missing, though. She did need to explore the facility's kitchen a bit more, and carefully. It had a side door she'd be leaving through, and Lydia held her breath as she crept to the now empty cooking space. She'd decided to escape through this door during the early morning; she was known for sneaking into the kitchen and snacking when she wasn't supposed to, so she hoped that if she were caught, she'd have a believable excuse for her presence in the kitchen. But, Lydia had never actually examined the alarm systems in the room. She wanted to go in, get some information, get out, and maybe even mess with the security cameras a bit in preparation for the next day. But, to explore, she'd have to avoid setting off any alarms in the first place. The last thing she needed was extra angry scientists only twenty-four hours before her big mission. As Lydia moved stealthily through the room, she spotted something that froze her in her tracks: a door that was slightly, ever so slightly ajar. And although she knew it was stupid, although she knew that she should just keep moving and stick to the plan, she couldn't hold back. Such an opportunity of freedom hadn't presented itself before, and it was almost too good to be true, something out of a dream. She feared that if she didn't move quickly, she would lose her chance. Her sudden instinct to feel the wind and the sun and the wide-open space clicked into place, and her focus kicked into high gear. In that moment, Lydia was immensely grateful for her hobby of stealing money from the scientists; she could feel some of that stolen cash in her pocket right now. Lydia looked over her shoulder one last time. She slinked to the door, placed her hand gingerly upon it, pushed it further ajar...

"Hm." A short sound escaped her lips, and she came to a halt, peering around her to make sure no one had heard. She hadn't expected it to be so...easy; she'd expected an alarm to start blaring, echoing off the walls and screaming "LYDIA IS LEAVING!!!" She wondered if she actually should just leave today. The sandy expanses of Arizona that surrounded the facility seemed to be calling to her, begging her to escape while she still had the chance. Mrs. Tyren would be back any second, ordering her around. Lydia made up her mind. Slipping out the door, she gazed out towards the tan landscape and wondered where the road might be. But a sweaty hand clamping over her mouth cut off the thought.

A face swung into view, the eyes bulging. Suddenly, Lydia was on her back, and she scrambled to stand up, getting her feet under her only to be thrown to the ground again. Spitting onto the dirt, she was surprised to see splotches of blood, and she felt her face to check for the injured spot. As she pulled her fingertips away from her face, crimson droplets fell from her cheek. Already, a new plan had formed in her head: Beat the living crap out of this guy and leave before he could catch up with her.

"This is my one job," a harsh voice spat out. It reminded Lydia of venom. "And I won't be liking the source of my job leaving, now will I?" The man leaned down to whisper into Lydia's ear. "So, how about you get back in there and we'll both pretend this never happened?"

Lydia had never heard this voice before, but she knew the man must work in the facility. Heart pounding, she summoned all her energy and strength for a fight.

"You're right...we *will* pretend this never happened" Lydia shot back, swinging her arm on the last syllable to elbow the man's face right next to her ear. He fell back in shock and, scrunching up his face, he bound towards her. But before he could swing again, she was up and sprinting, not daring to look back. Lydia could hear his footsteps in the sandy dirt close behind, but she continued to run.

"Trust me, you don't wanna do this! The people, they'll use you! They'll capture you, keep you for money!"

"Sounds familiar…kinda like how you used me, right?" she barked. His footsteps faded, and suddenly, it seemed like she was in the middle of nowhere. Sure, she was a day early on leaving. But she was free. An indescribable feeling bloomed in her chest, taking form and making her feel unstoppable. She ran and ran and never stopped.

That is, until she tripped, tumbling down and down into a smooth metal chamber. A green wave shot out of the sides as she fell. The ceiling above sent a pulse of electricity her way, knocking her further towards the ground. The facility had done their job and done it well. Metal shifted and closed in on both sides of the pit, sliding into place rapidly until only a square of the sky was visible. To Lydia's right and left, the metal curved, and she realized that she was stuck in a trap that circled around the entire facility like a moat. Her back ached horribly as she slid against the edges of the wall. Finally reaching the bottom with a loud thud, Lydia clambered to stand up. Surveying the chamber, Lydia felt along the walls for some sign of a door. As her palms slid along the shiny metal, she caught sight of her face in the reflecting surface. Blood oozed from a jagged cut along her cheek, and her arms sported scratches that ran from the shoulders to the wrists.

Lydia backed away from the reflection, evaluating her options. The metal was completely smooth, so she couldn't grab onto it and climb, and there weren't any tunnels leading out of the pit. The top was too high to jump for, and the shooting pain in her leg warned her not to try. It seemed impossible to escape without waiting for the man to catch up with her. Slowly, a plan began to form in Lydia's mind, but she knew how risky it was, how unlikely it was to go as she hoped.

Finally, the burly man arrived, staring down into the pit through the small square that had a view into the world above. His eyes lit up with laughter as he examined Lydia. She suddenly felt like an exhibit at the zoo, and the man was a child, ogling at her through a thick sheet of glass.

"Look what you did now," he jeered. "I can't wait to tell them all that I caught you. Maybe even get some extra money in my paycheck."

Nausea shifted through Lydia's stomach. Trying to ignore his jabs, Lydia focused on the task at hand. "Alright…you won. Now get me out of here," she demanded. "Throw me a rope," Lydia sneered, crossing her arms.

Unable to deny that he needed to find some way to get Lydia out, he retreated to fetch a thick rope from the facility.

While he was gone, Lydia sat, her back resting against the walls. Grazing her hand along her skin, she felt the burns that the slide had made and the scratches she had received from her landing. Her legs felt like twigs after hitting the ground, and she rubbed her sore knees. It felt like an eternity passed while Lydia waited anxiously for the time to take action. She shoved the heels of her hands against her forehead, pushing away the headache that raged above her eyes.

The sun beat down relentlessly. Lydia squinted around the trap, searching for an inkling of shade. She cringed when there was none to be found.

After some time, the man finally returned, throwing a rope down to her. "If you try anything," he threatened, "you'll pay for it." He planted his feet firmly against the ground far from the edge of the pit, digging his heels deep into the sand. He scrutinized Lydia as if she were a wild bear. Finally, he lowered the rope.

Grabbing hold, Lydia felt herself rise into the air. As she neared the surface, a burst of energy rocketed through her. Her blood pumped quicker, quicker, until she reached the edge of the opening. Abruptly, she yanked as hard as she could on the rope with her left hand, grabbing hold of the edge of the metal with her other. The man came tumbling down beside her, rolling into the pit. Relief flooded through Lydia until she felt him grab hold of her leg, weighing her down. Her hands slipped, and her foot waved through the air as she struggled to climb out of the pit. The sweat on her fingers made her grasp on the metal slip, and every centimeter they moved, every minuscule shift in her hold instilled a deeper hysteria in her heart. Lydia kicked her leg backwards and connected with the man's face. The guard let go as his head whipped in response to her foot.

Lydia scrabbled out of the pit, her hands raw from the ordeal. By now, her palms burned after pressing into the sun-soaked metal and she could feel the sharp ache in her back. Limping away from the edge on her weakened legs, Lydia could see a road far in the distance. It beckoned to her, begging her to run faster. She could hear the guard swearing at her, and afterwards, the soft static of a walkie talkie. There were only two directions: backwards, to a scarred past, and forwards, to an uncertain but hope-driven future. Lydia flung herself towards the latter desperately. Mustering up the little bit of strength she had left, she ran towards the road and ignored the shouts coming from the metal chamber. Finally, the facility was behind her, and she hoped it would be something she would never need to think about again. Her legs carried her further and further from the white building, further and further from the pit and the memories. As she ran, the road came into clear view and she began to trot beside it, resting her legs. Lydia slowed to take some breaths. It was only a matter of time before the other guards would catch up with her, and she needed to think fast. Continuing to run after her short break, she realized that she had to get as far away from the facility as possible.

# CHAPTER EIGHT -- EMILY

Emily winced at the word that had just escaped her mouth. When had she ever said "no" before? Cringing at the thought of what Linda must look like, she opened one eye and took a quick glance at her face. It was crimson, a deeper red than Emily had ever seen before. But what surprised her the most was the genuine look of…was it sympathy? No, it was disappointment, and it showed the most in her eyes.

"Oh, I knew it would come to this one day," Linda scowled, her face fading back to a shade of lighter red, a more familiar one. Circling Emily like a vulture, she slowly shook her head. "How selfish, how immature of you, to refuse to do the simple tasks you've been doing all your life. You have a gift that needs to be capitalized on."

Emily shook her head violently, jumping up quickly and facing Linda head on. Her heart was pounding, her head throbbing, every piece of her burning into flames and engulfing her. "It is not selfish. You don't need living power plants. This is all for convenience! Why do you need so much energy? Can't you live with just a little less?!" A tear trickled down Emily's cheek, but she wiped it away before Linda could notice. All the hurt and pain combined to form a volcano, and that volcano was finally erupting. "You stole our lives! What about my parents? What about…what about my friends?"

Linda's response split Emily's heart in two. "You're technically property of the government, now. Your parents took home a beautiful baby girl from the foster system the day you were born. They never suspected a thing."

Emily stopped moving for a moment. The world came to a halt. "What...what do you mean? My parents, they don't miss me—they don't know me?"

"We're much more powerful than you think, Emily. The government just did a swap—a baby from the foster system for you."

"You...you're...you're sick!" Emily shouted, preparing to smash her window and escape. She didn't care that it was a day early. She just knew she had to get out before she did something murderous.

Linda continued to frown, cocking her head. "Don't you see? This is all you have. It's all I have, now," she laughed softly, almost disbelievingly.

Finally, something deep within Emily snapped. Rushing towards Linda, who stepped back in confusion, she shoved her out the door, knowing it would only gain her a few seconds. Linda fell on her back, shock spreading over her face. Emily pushed her dresser up against the door. Threats spilled out of Linda's mouth as she viciously jiggled the doorknob. Emily's eyes urgently darted around the room, settling on the lamp on top of her night stand. It was solid and big, perfect for what she planned to use it for. She rushed towards the window and smashed it with all her might until a minuscule spider web appeared in the glass. The cracks grew and grew until the window shattered, sending shards of glass flying. Aware that she would be cut bloody, but willing to take the risk, Emily hoisted herself onto the sill and squirmed through the window just as an alarm sounded behind her.

Emily could feel the jagged glass already drawing blood, but she kept wriggling until she was completely out of the window frame. Rain poured onto her face. The sky screamed in fury, clouds gushing water and splitting with lightning. Stumbling to her feet, Emily darted away from the building as fast as she could, slipping every few yards but righting herself almost immediately. Puddles doused her shoes, freezing her toes and soaking her socks. But that was the least of her worries. Bellows sounded to her right, at least a dozen people yelling, while frantic footsteps grew closer to her left.

To Emily's dismay, a motor revved up in the distance, screeching along the paved road that ran throughout the facility. Its noise grew until it sounded like a chainsaw was drawn right next to her. A truck finally swerved in front of her, eight people with tranquilizer darts inside and aiming to shoot her legs. She spun around, scouring for an escape, but couldn't find any. Desperately, Emily backed up, shaking in the coldness and dripping wet.

"Take it nice and easy and no one will get hurt, alright?" The man in the front of the group offered his hand to her. He sounded amiable, gentle.

Emily knew better. Already turning on her heel, she lurched the other way, glaring over her shoulder all the while to watch the group. But her path was cut short when she crashed into Linda, a smile slowly spreading across her face. Gripping Emily's shoulders, she wheeled her around to face the guards with the tranquilizers, all of whom were carefully watching her.

"Let me go!" Emily screamed, twisting under Linda's tight grasp.

"Shoot her. Now. She cannot leave."

Emily's eyes widened. Her knees wobbled beneath her. But before she could move, a dart plunged into her right leg. It only hurt for a second, her body fading into numbness, the ground in front of her shifting. The world was already leaving her eyes, everything turning gray and then black, darker and darker until all was gone.

And she was out.

# CHAPTER NINE -- MITCH

Mitch could hear his heart beating off rhythm as he watched through the window, where the girl he had seen earlier was sprinting towards the gates that surrounded the facility. She darted like a wild animal.

Knowing he would only slow her down by trying to catch up, he decided to distract his mom, whom he heard storming down the hallway. When Mitch had seen the scientists' most recent experiment, he had adamantly refused another chance to be tested, disgusted with what they did to the girl named Emily. Since then, he'd waited, hoping for a chance to help her, the guilt of his mother's actions weighing on his soul. Besides, Mitch actually kind of liked her, thought she was smart and strong.

Mitch had heard a crash, and then the sound of an alarm. A moment later, he spotted her running outside.

Under pressure, all he could think to do was pretend Emily had decided to return and attack him in her anger. Slamming his door, he began to scream, "No, Emily, please don't!" Mitch heard his mother hurry down the hall, but knew she only cared about finding the girl, not whether he was hurt or not.

"Mitch, I'll have you severely punished if you pull an antic like that again!" she sputtered, appearing in the doorway, obviously disappointed at the absence of Emily attacking him.

"It wasn't an antic, she ran down the hall!"

Pushing past him, his mother stared out the window and gaped at Emily, who was still stumbling through the downpour. She threw him out of the way as she left, fuming.

The rest of the scene played out like a movie before his eyes. He flinched when the truck pulled in front of Emily, winced when she tried to run again. He was compelled to watch as she was shot by a tranquilizer dart and dragged into the facility, her face so quiet and innocent it burned his heart.

He sat still, in a trance for almost three hours. His eyes rested on the spot she had been hit. Although he stayed completely still, ideas were somersaulting through his mind.

Mitch was sure of what he had to do, knew where they must have taken her. The facility was the only playground he'd ever explored; Mitch had examined every nook and cranny of it.

He crept down the hallway to the operating room, spotting the security guard that always kept watch over the section. Pressing himself against the wall, he peeked around the corner and watched as the man pulled a pack of cigarettes out of his pocket. He fumbled for his lighter, glancing around the hall. The guard peered at his watch and then at the nearest exit. Shaking his head, the guard stepped out the door, muttering to himself, "Goddamn smoking ban…I've gotta quit."

Mitch peered at the operating room. He looked at the exit that the guard had gone through. Back, and forth. This was his one shot.

Mitch moved as quickly as he could to the operating room door, staying in the shadows. Slipping through the door, Mitch gasped. Emily was strapped to the metal gurney, pale-faced and unconscious.

It was then that he knew for sure.

He had to save her…somehow, someway.

# CHAPTER TEN -- EMILY

Light surged through Emily's heavy eyelids, too dazzling in the dank room she lay in. The bed squealed under her movements, the wheels on the bottom scratching across the floor piercingly enough to wake Emily up a bit.

She was only partially aware of what had occurred, of why she was stuck in this room on a metal bed. It wasn't until she tried to lift her hand to smooth the hair out of her face that she discerned that both of her wrists were strapped down to the gurney. A cramp in her head twinged with each movement, swelling to a steadier pulse as she gradually came to.

Emily tried to sit up, only to realize that a strap held her chest to the table as well. She groaned. Still recoiling from the vivid light, Emily blinked over and over, observing the circular room that enclosed her. Splotches of blue and black floated wistfully through her vision, blocking out the dingy walls. If she listened closely, she could detect faint voices in an adjacent room.

Hearing Linda's hisses next door sent a jolt through her and brought the memories of previous hours crashing into the void that was her brain. Tranquilizer, darts, Linda, run, window. Unsuccessful escape, held against her will, falling fast asleep. They were ingredients for a complex mixture Emily liked to call hatred, and she knew the poison of it was filling her at that very moment. She would never let them use her again. But she had to wait for the right moment to attack, the perfect opportunity.

***

The doorknob squeaked as someone on the other side shoved the door open. The person who entered was the boy from the gym. His eyes darted back and forth: door, Emily, door, metal bed, door, Emily.

A few coughs pierced the air, startling Emily out of her stupor. Her heart accelerated when he spoke.

"Look, I'm really sorry. About everything. But trust me, I didn't choose to live here." He spoke as he worked on undoing the straps that held Emily down.

"Wh-what do you mean?" she stuttered, narrowing her eyes, digging through his for the truth. Who was this kid? And why had she never talked to him before today, before the gym? Emily bit her tongue to keep from speaking aloud. Maybe, if she'd known him, she would have had a friend through the years. Even more than sadness, anger grew within Emily. How could the scientists keep him from her? She couldn't help but think of the wasted time; the lost friendship.

"My mom. I bet you know her, right?" He didn't wait for Emily to respond. "Yeah, well I was born here, sort of a mistake, I guess. My dad walked out, my mom refused to accept the fact that she was pregnant, and what do you know, one day her stomach is growing. But, she refuses to leave work, goes into labor, and hey! we've got docs here to do it all."

"Why are you telling me all of this?" Emily rubbed the pain out of her newly freed wrists. Her chest was still bound to the table, but Mitch had almost undone the straps on her ankles.

"Because I want you to know that I don't like what goes on here, but I can't leave now, not after all this. I've already seen too much here, and this is my home, I guess. I did refuse to support their work, so my days pretty much consist of me sitting around, waiting for something to change."

Emily's face twisted into a slight grin, suppressing a laugh at the way he described his life. The feeling recoiled in on itself almost as quickly as it had come. Another question was nagging the back of her mind, and she couldn't ignore it any longer.

"Who is your mom?" she questioned, watching him shift his weight from foot to foot, noticing his ripped-up nail beds.

"Linda."

Emily marveled at the difference between mother and son.

"What's your name?" she barked at him. She winced at the callousness in her voice. Over the course of a day she felt like she had hardened, mind and heart and soul, into someone who doubted the world, someone who assumed that this boy must be another person sent to knock her down. She almost chuckled at the simplicity of the question, the fact that she had chosen to ask this one instead of the millions of other questions rolling through her mind; this could be her only chance to have them answered.

"Mitch." A sly grin appeared on his face, nearing goofy, as if revealing his true feelings about the facility gave him great relief. But the grin washed away when the door slammed open with Linda standing there, her eyes shooting red hot lasers at him.

He shrank in her presence, taking a few steps back.

"Michael!" she screamed, turning to the security guard behind her. "You idiot! How could let him get in here?"

But Michael hadn't been in the facility; Michael had been finishing up his smoke break.

Facing Mitch, Linda crept forward. "Mitch, you don't understand. She's fine, she's just learning how to—"

"No. She isn't fine. I hate it here, Mom. I hate what you do to her."

And with that, Mitch undid Emily's last strap.

Emily stumbled off of the metal gurney.

In a split second, Linda was lunging towards her, tackling her to the ground. Mitch pulled on his mother's shoulders, throwing her off of Emily. Emily stumbled unsteadily to the wall, staring as Mitch held his mother down and yelled, "Go! Get out!"

But, before she began to run, she heard two words from Linda: "Shoot him."

They were strangled under the force of Mitch, but audible enough for the man outside the door to pull out a real gun.

"NO!" Emily pleaded. Before she could try to push the gun out of aim, a bullet was whizzing through the air and Mitch toppled onto the ground beside Linda. Emily rushed to him, gawking at the blood that gushed from the bullet wound.

"She-she hit my arm. I think…th-think it went straight through, or…or only nicked me. Get out. I'll be fine." Mitch's eyes faded in and out of focus.

"No, you helped me, I help you. That's the rule. Now get up!" Grabbing his good arm, Emily propped Mitch onto his feet, where he immediately doubled over. Linda was already up, blocking the door.

"Don't waste another bullet on him. He's learned his lesson," she muttered.

"Shut up!" cried Emily, bolder than she had ever been. "Just shut up! You disgust me!" Stomping towards the tall woman, she raised her fist and smashed it into Linda's face. Emily heard a defined crack.

Linda crumpled to the floor, gripping her nose and trembling. Emily punched her again before she could stand, ensuring that she wouldn't be up and running for a while. The guard immediately raised his gun, aiming at them both.

"You wouldn't. You can't kill me, remember? I'm a Plug," Emily declared. For once, the thing that had ruined her life might just save it.

Realization passed over the gruff man's face, and he lowered his weapon and stepped away.

"Get behind me," Emily ordered Mitch. "To get to you, he'll have to shoot me first. And I know he can't do that."

Mitch obeyed, crouching behind Emily and sliding along the wall with her, all the way to the door.

Emily grappled with the doorknob. "Now we're leaving. You will be punished if you shoot me. But if you let me escape, you might have a chance. At least they'll have the possibility of finding me." She hoped he would let his fear take over, muffle his logic.

Emily and Mitch continued out of the door and sprinted down the hall, trying to put space between the operating room and themselves.

"Th-thanks," coughed Mitch, glancing at Emily.

An uncomfortable feeling washed over her, but deep down she liked how it felt, nervous and fluttery. The feeling left as quickly as it had arrived, and Emily refocused on their escape.

They twisted around a corner, hugging the edges of each bend.

"I feel awful," she whispered, shaking her head. "I can't believe I just did that. I punched someone. Twice." Emily felt ashamed, embarrassed to have been violent. But Linda deserved it; she'd shot Mitch. Anyways, it wasn't the time to think about that. They had to escape first. "Come on, we need to go. Let's head down this hall, there's a door to the left," she ordered, pointing up ahead. "Then we have to get the hell out of here, ASAP."

Mitch was faltering behind her, blood still dripping from his arm. "We? You're letting me come?" he smiled.

Emily argued with herself. Something inside of her wanted to bring him, thought it was only fair after he'd risked his neck for her. Plus, he could be helpful. But, he could also be dead weight. He might slow her down. She shook that thought from her mind.

"Of course," she answered, the decision final. She liked this kid. He didn't deserve to die.

"How can you let me? Aren't you upset that I'm the son of a woman who tortured you for years?' Mitch's eyes narrowed. He skidded to a stop, and Emily did as well, heart hammering in her chest.

"But it wasn't you, it was your mom and the P.E.I. You're two different people. Not everything runs in blood. Just because you're her son, doesn't mean you're the same person," Emily answered, meeting his gaze. "Now, c'mon," urged Emily. "The guards must be on their way by now."

He dipped his head in agreement, still holding his arm.

Emily peered at the bloody bullet wound. "We need money. And something to stop your bleeding. Do you know where your mom keeps her stuff?"

Mitch motioned down the hall and slipped past Emily. "Her room is near yours…I think I know where she keeps her money, but—"

"But, what?"

"If it's not there, then we'll just increase our chances of getting caught!"

"It's worth it. How are we going to escape otherwise?"

They continued to hurry down the hallway, finally reaching a doorway. Mitch jiggled the knob.

"It's locked!" His voice seemed to have risen three octaves.

"We'll need to break it down...c'mon." Backing up against the wall opposite the door, Emily motioned for Mitch to join her. "Alright...go," she commanded.

Together, they ran towards the door, slamming their bodies against the thick wood. Mitch grimaced on impact. The door only shook on its hinges, and they held their shoulders in pain.

"Again." Emily braced herself for the hit.

Suddenly, voices began to echo through the hallway. Then, the bodies they belonged to sped up.

"Come on! Again!" She urged.

Running at full speed into the door, Mitch and Emily tumbled through the threshold. The door flung open, swinging back and forth violently.

Scrambling to his feet, Mitch scrambled towards the bed, crouching to his knees and digging underneath it. Pulling out a thick metal safe, he began to enter number combinations.

"Do you know the password?" Emily was busy shutting the door. She dragged a chair and placed it under the knob to buy them some much needed time.

"I think so...9-23-49" Mitch whispered as the door of the safe swung open. "It's James'—my dad's—birthday." Emptying the safe's holdings onto the floor, he grabbed a stack of bills. Mitch peered up at Emily.

Emily ran to Linda's bathroom and ripped open the drawers, flinging open cabinets, searching for something to help Mitch. A thick roll of gauze sat in the back of the medical drawer, and she brought it over to him, wrapping his arm in layers and tying it off tightly. Mitch was lucky; the bullet had only nicked him.

Emily looked around the room, her eyes stopping on a wide window. She'd already made it through one window today. Maybe she'd get lucky again. "We've got to smash the glass."

Scooping up a small chair in the corner of the room, Emily moved towards the window, hurling the furniture against the glass with all her might. The glass shattered instantly, shards soaring onto the floor and the concrete outside. She placed her foot on the ledge of the window frame, hoisting herself up and landing on the opposite side of the wall. Mitch was already doing the same, Emily holding out her hand to help him through. As he landed on the ground outside, the door to Linda's bedroom swung open.

Emily's scanned Mitch's arm. She could see how much pain he was in and acknowledged that they needed a car, or some easier form of transportation than running. Observing the lot, she spotted one of the trucks they used around the facility to transport medical supplies and food. It was empty now, since the materials had already been dropped off, but there was a man under the vehicle with tools. Emily gasped; the key was still in the ignition.

As the alarm blared like the cry of a hyena, the man stood and rubbed his oily palms on his pants.

Emily grabbed Mitch by the hand and shoved him against the wall, inhaling short spurts of oxygen as her nerves took over. "We've got to get in that truck." Her words were clipped, and she counted silently to herself. She'd move in three…two…one… "Now!"

Emily and Mitch charged towards the doors of the truck, but the man noticed them too soon and stuck out his arm to stop them. Running straight into his forearm, Emily bounced back and held the part of her neck where she'd been hit.

Mitch glanced between Emily and the man anxiously, finally breaking out of his stupor and elbowing the man with his good arm.

This only angered the truck's driver, and he punched back.

Mitch rocked on his heels, losing his balance.

They were running out of time. Desperate, Emily looked at the truck. A wrench rested on the hood, slick with oil from the man's hands.

Lunging for the wrench, Emily swung around, smashing the tool against the man's head. He stumbled back and hit the ground hard, his head knocking against the pavement. He was unconscious. Emily crouched over his limp body and searched for a key card; she'd noticed the gate's lock system earlier, during her first escape attempt. Shuffling through his pockets, she pulled out a small laminated card with his identification and job typed across its shiny surface; he was a mechanic.

She shouted at Mitch to get in the truck, and flinging the driver door open, he jumped in and reached his hand out for Emily. She gripped it gratefully, moving quickly away from the now awakening man and climbing into the passenger seat. Mitch revved the engine and slammed on the gas. The engine burst to life like thunder. He brought them veering through the lot, past the parked vehicles. They pulled up to a small scanner, and Mitch pressed the key card against it. Almost instantaneously, the gates began to creak open. Mitch and Emily sped down the road leading to their new lives.

"We made it, Em. Can I call you that?" Mitch gasped, out of breath.

"We almost made it," Emily numbly corrected him, heart pounding in her chest. Twisting in her seat, she glanced back at the facility and allowed herself to take in the moment completely. Emily sank into her seat. Her mind couldn't fully grasp that she was free.

"So, um, where exactly are we going?" Mitch interrupted her trance.

"A train station. Do you know where one is? They'll be able to follow us if we stay in this truck."

To Emily's surprise, he answered with a "yes."

"How do you know where a train station is if you've always lived at the facility?" An unusual cloud of suspicion rose within her as she looked over at his dark face.

Shaking his head, Mitch frowned. "I've tried to get out before…that was the farthest I made it."

"Oh…I'm sorry." Looking down at her folded hands, she let out a deep breath. They'd actually done it…well, not yet…they still had to catch a train to Topeka without being caught.

After another thirty minutes, Mitch and Emily pulled into a dingy restaurant parking lot and dashed out of sight. The train station wasn't far off now, and Emily's nerves were higher than ever. She couldn't imagine coming so far only to be caught again.

Only a few people raised their eyebrows at the two sprinting teens.

Emily hurried Mitch along. "We haven't made it yet," she warned. Her hair clung to her forehead, eyes wild with anticipation.

They sprinted the last mile to the station, finally reaching it and preparing for the long ride.

The tickets used up a large part of their money, but they bought them at the booth hastily and sped to their boarding section. As they settled into a pair of seats to wait for the train, Emily allowed herself a sigh of relief.

"Sure," she managed to whisper, out of breath as she rubbed her forehead.

"Sure, what?" Mitch gripped the armrests of his chair, fingernails digging into the cheap cushions.

"You can call me Em."

"Oh…thanks," he chuckled unsurely. Still, his hands relaxed on the armrests.

# CHAPTER ELEVEN -- TROY

"Nice seeing you again, Troy," murmured the tall man named Mr. Filroy who had emerged from the shadows. His footsteps echoed off of the walls.

Finally unmasked from the shadows, Troy had a clear view of his face. Heavy creases appeared next to Mr. Filroy's eyes, dark circles below them that shone with sweat. His bottom lip was peeled raw, as if he had been biting at it for days.

The man's gruff voice boomed, exploding through the entire room. "So…I've been hearing about an escape over in Tuscon and an attempt in Duluth, is that right?" The man's eyes were unfocused, his pupils shifting in size so rapidly that Troy became dizzy. Mr. Filroy blinked, backing into the shady corner once again.

Heavy breaths came from the darkness, a dread in them that sent goosebumps up Troy's arms. Something was wrong. Usually, despite being cold and stern, the doctor was completely focused, trying to make it through the maintenance appointment as efficiently as possible. But today, he was the opposite. At the same time, Troy's lips curled into a smile at the doctor's mention of Duluth and Tucson. Happiness beyond measure erupted for Lydia, but sympathy and fear for Emily also cascaded through him. She couldn't have been successful in her plans if Mr. Filroy only regarded her escape at the Duluth facility as an "attempt." He only hoped that the news would not travel as quickly to the other facilities, hoped that no extra means of security would be put in place. But, he didn't have time to ponder the thought.

"No, I haven't heard anything," he vowed, trying his best to keep the excitement out of his voice.

Instantly, the man burst out of the shadows, saliva flying from his mouth. He rushed to Troy, who fought to free himself from the man's steely grip.

"IF I LEAVE, THEY'LL KILL ME! DO YOU HEAR ME? AND IF YOUR FRIENDS DON'T GO BACK, IF THE TEST FAILS, ALL OF THE WORKERS THERE WILL BE KILLED, TOO! I AM STUCK HERE…TRAPPED." Mr. Filroy jostled Troy, insanity creeping into his twitching face. "THE GOVERNMENT CAN'T HAVE US TELLING THE WORLD ALL WE'VE DONE TO YOU! THERE ARE STILL SOME PEOPLE OUT THERE, PEOPLE WHO DON'T AGREE WITH OUR METHODS. THOSE PEOPLE ARE IGNORANT, THEY'LL TURN AGAINST US. THEY'LL TRY TO SAVE YOU, TRY TO DESTROY US! THE GOVERNMENT WILL KILL ME…THEY'LL KILL ME IF I TRY TO GET OUT!" He backed away, tremors shaking his body.

Troy sat frozen. He had never heard of the P.E.I. killing people before. His life had been awful, being hooked up to machines, being forced to complete strenuous tests all for the sake of an experiment, but he couldn't believe that the government would hurt its own people. A new idea was taking form in his head. Sure, he had to escape, but he couldn't let these workers die because of him, no matter the mistakes they'd made or the things they'd done. First, he needed to get Mr. Filroy under control, maybe help him gain some clarity. He jumped off the table, grabbing the wrists of the doctor.

"Hey, I won't let them" whispered Troy, checking that the door was closed.

Mr. Filroy gradually quieted, his breaths easing to a steadier pace. He raised his eyes to meet Troy's. "You can't stop them. How would you, even if you had the chance?" he grimaced, a tone to his voice more bitter than Troy had ever heard.

The statement sent a shiver through Troy, but he shook away the doubt. "I'll..well...I don't know. But I'll figure it out. Just give me a minute."

He sat in the corner, scrunched up his forehead, and held his head in his hands. Troy began to think of a way to fix everything. He asked himself what was most important to the facilities. Money? Power? The whole situation felt blurry in his mind, making it nearly impossible to concentrate. But over time, one word repeatedly appeared in his mind: Plugs. He and his friends. That must be what they cared most about. Without them, the test wouldn't be alive and running, there would be no power, no money. Now, he only had to figure out a way to use that to his advantage. But how? Troy could hear Mr. Filroy pacing, his nails picking away at the remainders of each other.

Troy rubbed the back of his neck, a move he often performed when pondering. He was lost in thought, grasping in the dark for some saving grace, when his finger brushed the cool metal implant in his shoulder. All of the Plugs had one—a metal sensor called a plug that transferred the energy from their bodies to large machines that harnessed and converted that energy into electricity. But Troy didn't care about the use of the plug—he cared about the dangerous location of it. In order to transmit the energy from their DNA, the implants had been attached to essential arteries in each of the Plugs' bodies. And this meant that the removal of the plug was equivalent to death.

Troy suddenly gasped.

Mr. Filroy shot him a glance. "What?!"

"Are...are you the only one who knows how to do this? These inspections, I mean."

"I've been here from the beginning, and I'm the only one who's currently trained for it. They'd have to take years to teach another, and they'd need all my files and notes and..."

"So, they don't want to lose you?"

"No, I suppose not," Mr. Filroy announced with an air of pride.

Troy rolled his eyes. "Well…let's make them think they're going to lose you, then."

# CHAPTER TWELVE -- LYDIA

The paved road was empty. Heat rolled across the ground in waves, drifting over Lydia's shoes while sweat ran down her face. The sun bore into her numb and weary muscles. With each pound of her feet, pain throbbed up her legs.

When Lydia staggered over a rock for the fourth time, she moved to crouch by the side of the road. She needed to think…how would she reach Topeka from here? With no way to call for help, Lydia felt that there was only one way to reach the city.

As she stood up, her legs shrieked in protest. Ignoring the new discomfort, she held her arm out and tilted her hand, pointing her thumb away from the facility. Lydia silently scolded herself. If only she'd waited…then maybe she could have stolen more money, even a car. She'd learned time and time again that instincts got people hurt, instincts were nothing but a distraction from logic. So how had she allowed her impulse to take over her actions so completely and irrevocably? More importantly now, how long would it take for someone to pick her up?

Apparently, hours. The sun shifted to the center of the sky, glaring down onto the uncovered road. Lydia flopped down again, the heat gnawing at her. Aches tore into her ribs, splintering deeper with each breath. Everything was starting to feel hopeless. In the ruthless heat, her brain shrugged forlornly and gave up for the day; no more coherent thoughts, no more reasoning.

Lydia grappled with the desire to collapse right then and there. She registered how easy it would be to find her, wandering around near a lonely road within miles of the facility. Pushing herself from the curb, she went on.

After another hour, she came upon a tall sign with a truck symbol pasted on it. Leaning against the blistering metal pole, she waited. Lydia couldn't help but berate herself. She should have waited for a better time to bolt, given herself more time to prepare. She dropped her head into her hands.

Water flooded her thoughts. Lydia yearned for arctic water, water flowing down her torrid throat, water seeping from the tippy top of her head to the edges of her toes. The fieriness of the day muddled her thoughts. How long had it been since she'd left the metal trap? Lydia blinked at her palms. They were still blistering from the escape. It hurt to curl her hands into fists. When was the last time she had sipped any fluid at all? She recalled the morning breakfast and the soda. Oh, God, how much Lydia would give for a drink of water or soda or anything right now.

She jumped at the rumbling of a vehicle in the distance. It turned a corner, and through the haze she could see large wheels coming closer. Hopping up and down, Lydia wave her arms, hoping to catch the driver's attention. The truck slowed to a stop in front of her, the window rolling down. A gust of cold air rushed from inside.

"What?" The driver hollered down towards Lydia.

"I need to get to Topeka…are you going east?" Lydia rummaged through her pockets, whipping out an untidy wad of cash and waving it like a referee.

The driver eyed the cash, eyed Lydia's flushed and swollen face. "Well, yeah, I'm heading east, but not all the way to Topeka. I'm going to Willard."

Lydia sagged with relief. Finally, she could be on her way to find her friends. "Sounds great," she shouted up towards the window.

Motioning with her head towards the passenger seat, the driver unlocked the truck.

"Alright, come on, then. The shipment is due tomorrow night."

Lydia climbed into the passenger's seat and slammed the door. It was time to leave. Get to Willard and hitchhike again. She was grateful for the lucky break.

The driver seemed to think so too, muttering, "You're lucky I picked you up."

# CHAPTER THIRTEEN -- TROY

"That will never work," Mr. Filroy spat, glaring at Troy as if he had committed some unforgivable atrocity.

"I have a plan. You want to get out, right?"

"Yes, but there's no—"

"And you'd do anything to be free?"

Mr. Filroy raised his eyebrows. "Well...yes, I guess..."

"Then, listen. You're going to play my hostage. Then, at least you have a choice once I'm free...you can come back if you get too scared or leave for good. Just fake it for ten minutes, get me out of here, and you'll never have to worry about me again."

Glancing at the door, Mr. Filroy gnawed on his lip. He rubbed his eyes, cracked his knuckles.

"So, what do you say?" Troy pressed.

And then, Mr. Filroy looked at him with such a burning ferocity that Troy moved an inch back. "I'm in. What do I need to do? I don't want to have to say anything, I'll screw it all up and they'll figure us out."

"I'll do all the talking," Troy assured him. "We just need a weapon, something they think I can hurt you with."

Mr. Filroy reached over to the cart. It was filled with all of the tools Mr. Filroy would've used for Troy's examination. He picked up a scalpel, handing it over to Troy.

Reluctantly, Troy wrapped his fingers around the scalpel. He felt dirty just holding it. "Alright. The act begins now, then."

Troy slammed the door open, wrapping his arm around Mr. Filroy's neck in a headlock and dragging him towards the nearest exit. He hobbled under his weight, shouting at Mr. Filroy to scan his key code for the rarely-used exit.

A scientist peered out of their office, screaming for help. "GET OFF OF HIM, TROY! COME BACK NOW! GUARDS!"

Troy only held the scalpel closer to Mr. Filroy's neck.

A crowd started to gather, guards whipping around the corner with tranquilizer guns.

"Shoot, and I kill him!" Troy waved the scalpel around in the air. His knuckles were white around the weapon.

Mr. Filroy kicked out with his feet, appearing helpless.

Troy let the tip of the scalpel touch Mr. Filroy's neck. A dribble of sweat dropped onto the metal.

"I'll end him," he hollered at the guards one last time. Troy pushed Mr. Filroy towards the door, keeping an arm around him. Yelling loudly enough for the guards to hear, Troy ordered the doctor to scan his card again.

"HURRY!" Troy screamed.

The lock buzzed, and Troy swung the door open.

The guards were nearing, growing impatient. They held their tranquilizer guns out in front of them, trying to find a good angle to shoot at Troy, but failing.

Troy pushed through the exit, Mr. Filroy close on his tail. As they turned the corner, they bolted towards a huge lot full of cars.

Troy pulled Mr. Filroy along behind him, sprinting towards the rows. "Unlock your car! GO!"

Mr. Filroy pulled out his keys, hitting the unlock button over and over. A car from one of the middle rows beeped, the lights flashing.

Troy and Mr. Filroy ducked between a silver car and a black one, staying hunched behind the hoods. Mr. Filroy's car was still thirty feet away. To get there, they would have to go through no man's land.

The same door they'd exited the facility with slammed open behind them, Mr. Miele begging Troy to turn back. There was actual pain in his voice, and for a moment Troy wondered if the man really did care about him after all. But he couldn't allow the thought to linger; it didn't matter anymore…he was getting out, now.

"We have to go!" Troy picked Mr. Filroy up from the ground, and they sprinted between the rows of vehicles, using them for cover from the onslaught of darts that were being fired their way.

Finally, they reached Mr. Filroy's blue car, Troy slipping into the passenger seat.

Sitting down in front of the wheel, Mr. Filroy turned the car on just as Troy slammed his door shut.

"Go, go, go!" Troy pleaded as Mr. Miele pounded on the passenger window.

The car swerved back and forth as they shot out of the lot, dodging between parked trucks towards gates in the distance. Reaching into his pocket, Mr. Filroy grabbed out his key card and pressed it against a scanning machine. The gates slid open in response, and they shot out.

The bulky trucks that the facility used were following close behind, and they sped up, two hundred, one hundred yards away, but the gates were already closing automatically. Troy held his seat tightly, nails digging into the soft leather as he watched the vehicles racing behind them. The guards were moving as quickly as possible, but the gate doors inched closer and closer towards each other.

For a brief second, Troy panicked. He screamed at Mr. Filroy to hurry, expecting the trucks to make it through the shrinking opening, but when they were thirty yards away, the gates shut with a deafening boom. One of the guards searched desperately in his jacket for a key card, giving Mr. Filroy time to hit the gas. The road curved in the distance, and as Troy watched behind him, he heard the gates open again. The car swerved, taking a sharp left just before the road bent; turn after turn, the doctor formed an untraceable path. Troy allowed himself to settle down.

"Thank you," he gasped, out of breath.

Mr. Filroy ignored him. "Give me the scalpel."

Troy obeyed, dropping the weapon into his hand. Mr. Filroy pocketed it.

Troy watched the road, the image of Mr. Miele limping after him stuck in his mind. He couldn't help but ask, "Do you know Mr. Miele?"

"Yeah," Mr. Filroy answered. "Pretty decent guy. Couldn't have kids of his own. He bragged about you to me…acted like you were his own child."

Troy's heart stopped for a moment. Clutching his head, he took a deep breath. "God, I'm awful. I'm so awful."

"What?"

"I left him back there. I left him all alone."

"Life is tough, kid. Sometimes you need to put yourself above everyone else."

Troy wasn't so sure he agreed.

After many minutes of taking unexpected turns and flying down side streets, Mr. Filroy somehow managed to emerge from the twisted, confused path he'd led the car through back onto the smoother road.

The ride had been awkward, tension thick in the air. But now, Troy and Mr. Filroy stood in an alleyway beside the train station, Mr. Filroy handing Troy a bit of money.

"You don't even know how much I appreciate this," Troy promised him.

"Actually, I do."

Troy frowned. "Where are you gonna go, now?"

A shrug. "I'll leave the state, maybe even the country…change my name. Maybe someday you'll see me on the streets and not even recognize me."

"Maybe. Well…good luck with that." Troy extended his hand.

Mr. Filroy shook it.

That was the last Troy ever saw of the doctor—or at least the doctor he knew.

Thirty minutes later, Troy was just relieved to have made it onto the train with the tickets Mr. Filroy's money bought him. The train wasn't too crowded, and Troy sat alone, with his jacket pulled tightly around him and his hood up. He was exhausted, but a massive part of him didn't want to let his guard down. So, he prepared himself for the long ride to Topeka, passing the time by filling his mind with memories.

# CHAPTER FOURTEEN -- EMILY AND MITCH
## TOPEKA, KANSAS

"It feels like we've been on these trains forever." Sitting back, Mitch cleared his throat. He was obviously growing impatient with all of the waiting.

"We have been." Emily sat with her arms folded, staring out the window at the cities and towns rushing by. "But there are only a few hours left. We're really early, so we'll have to find some place to sleep and eat." She felt like she was in a dream, something floating beyond the realms of reality. This was the longest she'd ever been out of the facility's grasp, and every new city felt like a glowing discovery.

By the time they reached Topeka, the sun was hiding behind the buildings.

The conductor announced their arrival over a loudspeaker as they passed under a metal sign, and Emily reached over to wake the now snoring Mitch.

"We're almost there," she grinned.

Mitch whooped in delight, but Emily shushed him.

"We're undercover, remember?!" She felt foolish saying it, acting like they were spies on some secret mission. But she didn't really mind sounding stupid in front of Mitch; he had a sweet sort of reserved smile that made her almost comfortable to act ridiculous.

As the train slowed to a stop, Emily and Mitch stood, hoping to exit unnoticed. Their entire trip had been new territory for them, and they prayed that everything continued to go smoothly. Stepping onto the concrete, they peered at the strip of lit up shops and restaurants. A factory in the distance spewed smoke into the air and made the sky a gray black for miles and miles. The moon was hidden behind smoke.

Emily's stomach rumbled, interrupting the foreign scene. She gave in to her stomach's protests willingly; she was starving.

"We need to find somewhere to eat…" Emily turned to the right, leading the way down the narrow walkway.

*** 

"Uh…we'd like to order something." Mitch's voice rang out against the small yellow walls and bounced off of the peeling linoleum floors.

Emily and he had managed to find a rundown sandwich shop with an OPEN sign hanging from a post on the window. Inside, a few men and women huddled around a television screen that was the size of a sheet of paper. An advertisement for an owl-looking animal called a Furby played on the TV. The little animal let out shrill noises while girls passed the toy back and forth. Emily cringed; she couldn't understand why kids would want a fake animal. She'd never seen anything like it.

Wandering around the room, Emily ran her hand along the smooth countertop, smelling the powerful disinfectant. A stack of menus sat meticulously folded on the edge of the counter. Glossy menu pages listed foods like sandwiches, pancakes, sausage, bacon, and waffles. Emily's mouth watered at the words. She couldn't remember the last time she'd eaten anything more flavorful than eggs.

Suddenly, a woman appeared at the counter with a notepad in hand. An apron was neatly knotted at her waist and she wore hot pink lipstick that didn't quite stay inside the lines.

"Um…hi, we'll just have two turkey sandwiches please," requested Mitch. He dug through his pockets for dollar bills.

Emily had to remind herself that he hadn't left the facility either—at least not for a long while. They were both discovering the world for the first time, together. That thought made her grin a little; everything was so new and fresh. She heard a song faintly playing in the background; something about a wannabe who needed to make some new friends.

The waitress held out her hand for the money, curling her shaky fingers around the paper bills. She shuffled away.

As the pair waited for their meal, paranoia began to creep into Emily's mind. What if there were guards watching them at this very moment? Was this some weird last supper for her? Maybe the scientists were already interrogating each other, trying to find some crack in the system or some mole that didn't even exist. The mere idea sent a shiver through her. Could their escape get other people in trouble? Emily felt a twisted form of happiness in her chest. She pushed it away in horror; revenge wasn't something she usually enjoyed or sought out. Besides…what if Mitch hadn't escaped with her? He might be in a tight room at this very moment, dodging every question that was thrown his way. Emily threw a look over her shoulder. She couldn't get rid of the feeling that someone was watching them.

In moments, the cashier trudged back to the counter and slid them a pair of sandwiches, interrupting Emily's train of thought.

Mitch and Emily picked up their food and found a table in the corner of the room. The disinfectant smell seemed a bit milder in the left hand corner of the restaurant, more of a whisper than a scream. Pulling out the screechy chairs, they sat down and dug in.

After a few bites, Emily started to think about how little they actually knew about each other. She wanted to really know Mitch, know his personality, his story, and she began to strike up a conversation.

"So, you lived at the facility your whole life?" Emily inquired. Shifting in her seat, she took another monstrous bite of her sandwich to avoid asking another question.

Mitch laughed at her; she looked like a chipmunk with all of the food in her mouth.

"Yeah, I lived at the facility. I've never really left, actually, so seeing new places is a first thing for me, too." He tore up a straw wrapper as he spoke.

"Oh, then we can experience it together, huh?" Emily's voice faded off, and she realized that she truly liked Mitch's company. She felt her cheeks turn red. He might be taken aback by her statement; had she gone too far?

"That's what we're doing already," smiled Mitch. Yet there was a hint of fear behind his eyes, and Emily could sense his nervousness.

"Are you scared? You know, of getting caught?" Emily placed her sandwich back on the plate and waited for an answer.

"I try not to be…but I can't help it. My mom would never forgive me if she found us."

Nodding, Emily stayed silent, thinking of the right way to respond to such a sincere confession.

"I think it's pretty amazing, you know. That you risked it all for your beliefs. It was brave of you." She took another huge bite.

Twenty minutes later, the pair had finished their food.

"We're here a day early, so I guess we need to find someplace to sleep. Any ideas?" Emily tossed her garbage in the trash can and stood up, motioning for Mitch to do the same.

"Not really…I'm not exactly a Topeka resident."

"Here!" Emily picked up one of the little folded maps on the countertop. Small squares and triangles littered the green and gray page, showing buildings and lodging. Emily tapped a blue dot. "How about this inn?"

"No way," Mitch laughed. "We'd be caught in a day."

"Then…do we have to sleep on a bench or something?"

"I really think that the forest around the cemetery is the safest place for now…I'm sure that the guards are looking for us, and if we're in sight of too many people, it could be bad," Mitch suggested. "Plus, the grass won't be as brutal as the cement."

"Alright…good idea. We're meeting the others at the Great Overland Station, though, so we need to get up early to look for them."

Moving towards the door, the two headed to the woods and prepared for a long night of waiting.

Mitch and Emily went further and further into the forest, the sound of cars disappearing behind the olive canopy. Now, the only noise was the rustling of their feet and the rhythm of their breaths.

Emily took it all in gratefully. How long had she waited for this?

Mitch peeked over at her.

"You look like you're on sensory overload." His laugh spilled out of him like honey.

"And you're not? I thought you'd never left the facility." Mitch's laugh made Emily grin and blush a little.

"Well, they let me outside sometimes, within the gates, of course."

"Hm." Emily couldn't help the jealousy that pounded in her chest. "That's…lucky for you."

"Yeah, I guess it is."

"You know, I feel kind of weird about all this."

"What?"

"About the fact that I still don't really know you that well at all. And we're kind of alone in the woods together. It's just…I don't know…"

"You know the big stuff. You know how I feel about the project, and you and your friends. You know my mom, and you know where I grew up…so that tells you a lot."

"That's true." Emily picked up a leaf and rubbed her thumb over its veins. The ridges felt nice on her skin.

"Linda's pretty awful, huh?"

"She's definitely, um…"

"Go ahead, you can say it."

"Fine, she's really terrible. But she's your mom. Don't you feel any connection with her?"

"She's family. That counts for something, I guess. But I don't think she'll ever really be my *mom*, you know what I mean?" All the terrible things she'd said to him, all the pain she'd caused, came flooding back in an instant. He remembered what he'd always thought: that words were just ripples, that the further they got from the center the less they meant. But he wasn't so sure anymore.

"I understand."

"Enough of this pity party crap. You want to know the little stuff?"

"Mhm. It's just as important as the big stuff, I think." Emily grinned.

"You're kind of right. So, what do you want to know?"

"Umm. Okay. What's your favorite food?"

A laugh escaped Mitch's lips. "I like spaghetti with marinara sauce, but I didn't get to eat it much at the facility."

"Mari...marinary?"

"No, no, marinara. It's red and..." Mitch closed his eyes. "It's so good."

"I've never tried it."

"I think I remember the recipe. I'll make it for you sometime."

Emily looked up quickly. "Thanks." A smile was in her voice.

"Alright, I get to ask now. What is your worst, most awful fear?"

Emily stopped for a moment. She dropped the leaf. Picked up a new one. "Never seeing the people I love again." Her voice was solid. Steady. Sure.

At first, Mitch didn't speak. "I thought you would say spiders or something. That's what I meant, at least, with the question. I'm sorry if I...you know...upset you."

"No, it's fine. Really. What's yours? Your real one, not some stupid cover one."

Mitch's eyes were blank. He stared past the canopy, past the trees, as if looking for something that only he could see. Finally he answered.

"No one ever loving me."

"I see. But, I don't think that'll happen. How could no one love you?"

"That's...really nice, Em. Probably the nicest things anyone's ever said to me, actually."

"I mean, I'm not trying to sound creepy, or whatever. I'm just saying, you're nice and all so—"

"No, no, it's okay." He let out a shaky laugh. "I shouldn't have been pessimistic in the first place. Sorry."

"Stop saying you're sorry for everything. It's fine. There's a lot I should be saying sorry for, too."

"Oh, yeah? Like what?"

"Like the fact that I probably just got thirty people fired by leaving the facility and screwing up the entire project."

"I thought you hated the Plugs Energy Initiative."

"I do. I really do, I swear. Still, I can't help but feel bad. The scientists…they gave up everything for this. They kept saying how important I was, how my life meant so much more than the average one. And I kind of just threw it all away. It makes me feel…I don't know, irresponsible? Immature, foolish? Does that make any sense at all?"

"Yeah. Yeah, it makes a lot of sense. I get it. But sometimes you have to be selfish, you know? You have to do what's best for yourself when it comes down to it."

"I guess you're right."

"Wow. I'm not usually right." Mitch snorted.

Emily let out a light giggle. "I usually am, so we make a good team."

"It's meant to be."

# CHAPTER FIFTEEN -- ANTONIA
## ALBANY, NEW YORK

Pain; it was the first thing Antonia felt when she opened her eyes halfway through her seventeenth birthday.

Waking up, she remembered the day before, how she'd tried to escape the facility while everyone slept. The halls had been dark as a black widow, the moon splattering the hallways with droplets of lights. Antonia thought of the locked doors, the hushed facility, the muffled snores.

But, when everyone did wake up, her face was broadcast across the news, and she was taken back to the facility by someone who needed the money the scientists had offered. She thought of the cloth in her mouth; the fabric that had turned her screams into little sobs.

The events after that had been a blur, mist that clouded her vision. And now, she was awakening in an unusual room, glass on all sides so that she could see each and every scientist observing her.

She spotted her reflection in the clear pane. Dark shadows encircled her eyes, and her hair stuck up in all directions. Her lower right lip was swollen, blood seeping out of it and down her chin. Scratches lined her arms, and her head felt fuzzy, as if full of static. Looking at her feet, she noticed that she lay on a metal table, her right arm securely clasped to it and both legs held down by metal as well.

"Antonia," drawled a scientist with a long face and a frown. "We are going to ask you one simple question. You can cooperate, or we will have to try some different ways to find your friends involving…painful consequences."

Feeling her voice tremble, Antonia asked, "What consequences?" She could practically hear her own heart beating. How had this all happened? How was she suddenly facing some type of unknown torture?

"The longer you take to answer, the more we will inject the serum into you. When you are ready to answer, hold up one finger. We are waiting," the scientist continued.

Nodding, Antonia tried to calm her nerves. She sucked in a lungful of air, then let it drift out slowly. There had to be a way out of this. Maybe she could weasel her way out of the predicament, use her smarts to figure something out.

A female scientist walked to the glass and began to speak, showing no emotion on her face. "We will only ask once, and I will not repeat the question, so listen clearly." Pausing for Antonia's nod, she continued. "Where, to your knowledge, have your friends agreed to meet?"

Antonia's heart shuddered. It felt like someone had grabbed her lungs and strung barbed wire around them, tying a neat little knot at the end. With every passing second, breathing grew more difficult. She listened with dread as the scientist warned her, implored her to tell the truth and avoid the pain, but there was no way she could betray her friends now.

The woman who had asked the question stepped through the door to Antonia's glass room and injected a needle into her left arm.

Suddenly, it felt like fire was making its way through Antonia's veins as the serum spread. After a moment, the pain came. Thoughts came in bursts of flame. Inferno swept through her vision, and the world shifted to a blazing scarlet. The back of her neck smoldered with vehement heat. Sweat poured down her face and dropped through her tangled hair. Trying to wrench her arm from the metal cuff, Antonia clenched her fists and screamed.

# CHAPTER SIXTEEN -- TROY

As the train moved further into the depths of the city, Troy's stomach twisted into tight knots. What if no one was there? What if he were the only one who had escaped? His nerves mounted, and along with them his senses heightened. Every smell, every movement, and every sound of the train magnified in his shaken mind. Even worse, the prying eyes of fellow travelers sent prickles down Troy's back. Their gazes lingered on his peeled nails and white knuckles.

The train finally pulled to a stop in the station hours later. Hundreds of people swept through Troy's vision, rolling suitcases behind them and heading in innumerable directions. Their shuffling feet left him dizzy.

He scanned the area for nearby guards. Pulling off his jacket, Troy stepped onto the platform and began to venture through the station to find an exit. His entire body felt as if it'd been torn up and clumsily sewn back together. Troy could only hope he would make it to the meeting point. Red exit signs glowed over the doors. Troy plodded along with the mob of people, holding his jacket to his chest like a shield. With his head bowed, he watched with downcast eyes as the exit grew closer. He thought of the metal sculpture he needed to reach; the safe haven he'd only ever imagined.

As he moved through the city, the sights came to his attention, one by one, until they painted a detailed picture of what life looked like in Topeka. The first thing he noticed were the shops lining the streets. There were families and children walking in and out of the stores, holding paper bags and soda cans. A big sign advertising a Nirvana concert hung in a store window. Next door, the theme song for a show called Seinfeld chattered along. Troy watched in awe. How did the world outside the facilities work? And what were concerts?

The buildings became fewer and fewer as Troy reached the narrower roads on the edge of the city. Paved sidewalks gave way to loose gravel, littered with weeds that poked out of cracks. Their little green tentacles slivered upwards, reaching for any opening they could find. The weeds reminded Troy of himself.

Trudging a little father, he searched the horizon for his destination. The paved roads started up again a few miles later. Warehouses sprouted up from the streets, and then little restaurants took their place. Troy's mouth watered at the smell of tacos. After six more minutes, he found the place.

A huge metal art piece loomed in the distance and two figures sat to the side of it.

Although Troy wanted so, so badly to run, he knew that he must practice caution. His hands quivered with anticipation, his lungs struggling for air. No one could be trusted in the real world, the scientists had told him. Maybe that was true. Maybe they had been right about one thing. Step by step, the people became clearer in his vision, and despite one of them being a boy whom he did not recognize, the other was a familiar face…definitely someone he knew. A few yards closer, and he could tell for sure. It was Emily.

He sprinted to her, joy surging through him. Finally, someone he knew and loved would be with him! Out of breath from sprinting the last few yards, Troy crossed the space between them and wrapped Emily into a tight hug. Troy could feel her shaking against his chest, her face pressed into his shoulder, and he buried his face in her hair to hide his tears. Moving her arm's length away from him, he broke into a wide grin.

"God, I've been waiting so long to see you," he breathed, hugging her back to him.

Her muffled voice reached his ears as she agreed. Breaking from the embrace, they stared at each other for a minute.

"You look so different…you're so tall…and you're so grown up," Emily said quietly, wiping her eyes. "But it's really you." She lifted her hand to his face for a moment, as if to feel that he was truly there. Searching his eyes, she seemed to decide that he was.

"I know, I know, I had a few growth spurts," he laughed. "Wow, I missed you so much, Emily. It's so nice to finally be together again…" Troy's heart began to slow as he relaxed.

"You too, Troy. How was your trip?! You need to tell me all about it."

"I will," he promised.

# CHAPTER SEVENTEEN -- LYDIA

Lydia was experiencing her next ride with a short man. He had graying hair and introduced himself as Frederick. The money she'd offered him for his services ruffled in the console.

Frederick kept taking shortcuts, winding through some back roads that drove through dense forest. His car reeked of smoke, old cigarette butts littering his floor. Frederick powered up the air conditioner and sent little puffs of dust shooting into Lydia's face. She sneezed on the dashboard.

In an obvious attempt to fill the new patch of silence, Frederick reached towards the radio, switching it onto the local news station and turning up the volume with a crackle. Heavy metal blared through the mediocre car speakers. Huffing in annoyance, Frederick muttered something along the lines of "dying lamb" and twisted the knob to change stations. Words came tumbling through the speakers, rapid and monotone. Frederick was about to switch the station again when the voice caught his attention.

It took Lydia a moment to comprehend the full meaning of the dull voice's words and string them together. It was when she realized that the news report was about the Plugs that she panicked.

The unfamiliar voice talked about a gang's supposed bank robbery and the reward for whoever gave information to their whereabouts, quickly listing off a description of each Plug.

Lydia rolled her eyes. Was the P.E.I. really pretending that the Plugs were a group of bandits?

The newscaster started with Lydia. "This young woman is approximately 5 feet, 8 inches, with dark hair and green eyes. She is 17 years old and was wearing black jeans and a gray jacket at the time of her escape. Can act aggressively and without thought."

Lydia huffed. Mrs. Tyren had definitely added that last part.

The reporter's voice continued to list off the appearance of each Plug. Lydia's heart beat faster and faster. Watching closely, she could see Frederick's eyes narrow as the gears in his head turned. His gaze shifted in her direction.

Time slowed down.

Frederick shifted his hand toward the lock button, and Lydia knew that this would be her only chance. Hurling her car door open, she catapulted onto the road. She rolled along the unforgiving ground, shoulders aching with the impact, and pushed herself up. Stumbling towards the trees for cover, she scanned the unknown terrain. Lydia needed to reach her friends and protect them...they were already being hunted down.

Frederick's shouts sounded from behind her, and she heard him stop his car and hit the ground at a sprint.

Lydia zigzagged through the murky forest. Sticks broke with her every step, and when she reached a tree with a thick trunk, she swerved, pressing her body against the firm bark. Panting quietly, Lydia peered around the tree and spotted Frederick twenty feet away. He lifted his feet gingerly, avoiding fallen branches. His eyes darted up and down, back and forth, passing over Lydia's hiding spot twice.

Panic flooded through her veins and she wrapped her arms around the wood, beginning to climb up the tree. Suddenly, her foot slipped, and a chunk of the wood tore away from the rest of the bark, clattering to the ground and catching the man's attention. Frederick stood stock-still and stared around him with the eyes of a hunter.

Knowing her own speed, Lydia sensed that her best hope was to start running. She jumped down from the tree, her hands skidding against the bark.

Frederick's gaze met her's, hunger pooling in his dark eyes. Abandoning all hope of surprise, he let his feet thud heavily against the ground as he ran.

Based off of Frederick's maps, Lydia knew that she needed to travel northeast to reach Topeka. She peered over to the road and checked which way Frederick's car was heading; they had been traveling northeast in the vehicle. She continued to run in the direction that the car's headlights pointed. Establishing a rough route for herself, she shot through the forest, fear fueling her speed.

The air rushed past her face painfully, and each breath blasted into her greedy lungs. She sucked down the cool air, feet pounding the ground with each step. She knew that she'd lost Frederick, but she couldn't will herself to slow down and rest. Her friends were waiting for her; Brice, Lydia, Antonia, Jared, Emily, Troy…she listed off the names in her head, repeating them like a mantra. The wind felt good against her cheeks, the tears smooth as they fled down her face in the sharp cold. Sometimes, it seemed like all she could do was run; run from the facility, run from her pain and her controllers. So, she kept going.

Lydia wasn't sure how long she'd been running when she reached her destination. She had trekked through the forest and eventually made her way into the center of the city. From there, she'd searched for the Great Overland Station, and she'd finally found it.

From behind a tree, Lydia observed four figures, each shifting to look at each other. The people's quiet voices carried towards her, and she listened intently, trying to make out their identities, but they were too far away. Thinking back to her car ride, she remembered the descriptions of each of the Plugs' escape outfits. They seemed to match those of these people closely enough. Taking a chance, Lydia crept behind them, hoping to keep as silent as possible until she could somehow see their faces. But as she moved, twigs cracked beneath her feet, and one of the boys in the group turned around. His red hair flew as he whipped his head to look at the source of noise.

Gasping, Lydia stood up straight and disregarded any precautions. It was Brice…she was sure of it. Jumping over the short stone wall and sprinting to the metal sculpture, she wrapped her arms around him and heard the voices of Emily and Troy as they realized who it was. They joined in the hug, creating a sort of huddle that Lydia knew must look ridiculous. But she didn't care.

# CHAPTER EIGHTEEN

As they all pulled apart, questions and cries of relief filled the air.

"What was it like in Arizona?"

"How'd you get here?"

"What happened when you escaped?"

Smiling broadly, Lydia motioned for them to stop their questions for a moment and sighed before answering. "Wait…who is this?" Lydia pointed at Mitch, staring him down. "No offense or anything."

"Well, it's kind of a long story," Emily began. "But he's okay, and you don't need to be afraid of him. I'll tell you everything once the others get here. First, you need to tell us about your escape."

"It was probably the same as what you all went through…I got here by waving down rides. There was this man, a guard, who trapped me in this sort of…I don't know, metal chamber or whatever. He started to take me out so that he could bring me back to the facility, but I pulled him into the trap, and that's when I got out of there." She couldn't bring herself to tell them about what she'd heard on the radio just yet, afraid of ruining the happy mood that had settled upon them. "But, it doesn't matter what happened after I left…" Her voice faded away. It hurt to accept reality…that they were still being hunted. That they weren't safe after all. The fact that they were on the news would certainly cause a disruption, and at the moment, Lydia wanted to simply cherish the reunion that she had waited so long for.

"A metal chamber? That's weird. I don't think we had that at my facility," Brice commented. "Maybe it was something new they were working on?"

"Like I said, who cares about their science fair projects? That's not something I want in my memory and—"

"Fine, fine. Then, we'll remember different things right now," Brice interjected. "Don't you remember when we hid from the scientists when we were younger, and they couldn't find us for a whole day?"

"God, how could I forget? I've honestly never seen them so angry, which kind of sucks, because I wanted to get the biggest reaction for my own stunt. Do you remember when I pretended to faint and then scared the whole facility?" Shaking her head, Lydia thought of the hilarious looks on everyone's faces...

"Wait, Emily, I just thought of this...There was that time we started a food fight, the scientists flipped out." Troy's eyes closed as he pictured the food flying.

And the memories continued to flow until it felt as if a day hadn't been spent apart.

***

"D'you think Jared and Antonia are on their way?" Emily mumbled through a mouthful of food as she snuck through the city with her friends.

"Of course they are," remarked Troy optimistically. "They're both smart...I'm sure they'll find their way here."

They had stocked up on food at a convenience store and were hoping to find someplace to stay for the night until the others arrived...but that was proving to be a difficult task.

Along the sidewalks, buildings sat side by side and the Plugs searched for a hotel. Yet, every time they did find one, it was too crowded with people and they feared that they would be recognized. The sun was beginning to set on the city, shining behind each building and disappearing as the moon took its place to watch over the skies.

"We've been away from the sculpture for too long. Someone else could've gotten here," Brice reminded them, leading the way back.

When they returned to the station, they spotted something that made their spirits soar. A single figure stood, silhouetted. It leaned against the stone base of the art piece and began to walk back and forth in a straight line, clearly under distress.

Twenty yards away, the Plugs advanced.

"Be careful!" Lydia shot her arm out, holding her friends back. "We don't know if it's him yet."

Emily sighed. "He's tall and lanky, he has brown hair, and he's pacing just like Jared used to. Relax!"

"No, Emily, Lydia is right," Brice warned. "We can't be seen or heard by outsiders."

Mitch turned bright red.

"Sorry, I didn't mean it like that, but, you kno—"

"Oh, just shut up!" Emily groaned.

Far in the distance, the figure turned. He had heard them.

Suddenly, the eyes of Lydia and the boy in the distance met. A second of recognition...a second of clarification. "It's him...it's Jared" Lydia uttered in disbelief. "Come on!"

And so, five figures ran towards one in the darkness until the six figures merged into one.

# CHAPTER NINETEEN

"Finally, you're here! We've been waiting all day," Emily breathed with relief as she pulled away from Jared.

"It's been so long since I last saw you all…" Jared's green eyes rested on each Plug as his smile widened, and then proceeded to fall. "Where's Antonia?"

Brice stepped forward to answer. "We're not sure…we think she'll be here later. If she doesn't get here soon, we'll have to find her."

Agreeing, Emily nodded. "We shouldn't stay out in the open for too long," she mumbled. Her eyes scanned the horizon. "C'mon."

Each of them walked away from the station entrance. Emily and Mitch led the way through the city to the cemetery they had stayed in the night before. No hotels had made the cut. They submerged into the trees' shadows. The trees were tightly packed, and the leaves overhead allowed only small slivers of light to reach the forest floor; other than those hints of light, everything was dark.

"How about here?" Troy pointed towards a small opening of trees whose leaves had almost completely fallen off, allowing more light to seep through.

"We're still too easy to spot here," grunted Brice.

As they crept through the trees, Jared explained how he escaped his facility.

"It was pretty hard," he explained. "That's why I got here kind of late. I had to use this one scientist who's always really liked me, and I asked him if I could go outside with a guard just to get some air. I walked through the door to the outside sector first, and by the time the guard had followed, I was sprinting. Then, I took a few buses. Now I feel kind of bad for tricking him. His name was Rick. He was always kind to me, but I had to get out. I think it was all an act anyways. Some sort of method to make me easier to control." A deep frown spread across Jared's face as he watched his feet. They kicked up piles of leaves.

Troy spoke. "I know how you feel. I caught my supervisor recording me the other day. Not a great realization that my only friend was just another guard," Troy laughed uncertainly. "I guess I really can't trust anyone besides you guys."

***

Dropping his backpack to the ground and kneeling beside it, Brice pulled out water bottles and food.

"Where did you get all of those?" Lydia crouched down and picked up a water bottle, opening its lid and gulping down half its holdings.

"I stole them back at the store…it's fine, we need them."

By now, the light had completely vanished from the sky and darkness seeped through the forest.

"You're right, but it still feels bad to steal," Emily sighed. "Whatever. I'll keep watch first." Moving towards a tree, she motioned for Jared to boost her up and started to climb to a higher branch. She needed a view of the sculpture; that's where Antonia would be.

"Wait, Emily! We've all asked you…who is the kid you came with? Can we hear the full story now?" Lydia's voice was tight and tense; trust was rare for her.

"Oh…um, Mitch. This is Mitch. He helped me get out of the facility. It's fine, you can trust him; I wouldn't be here if it weren't for his help. His mom actually shot him, but it only nicked his arm. We got really lucky."

Peering over at him, Emily smiled on the inside. She was more relieved than he knew.

A rosy tint filled Mitch's cheeks as he curled up at the base of the tree.

"Alright…well, thanks, Mitch," Lydia muttered. But, she kept her guard up. "Oh, I've been meaning to ask, how did everyone get here?! I know we heard Jared's story, but I want to know everything."

"Wait, wait," Troy laughed. "You're not going to believe this…you know the doctors who complete our maintenance checks each month? The ones who do our checkups? Well, mine got me out…he said he wanted to leave the facility, but they wouldn't let him because he 'knew too much,'" Troy motioned with his fingers. "Then, I took a train."

"Wait, are you sure it was your doctor?!" Emily's voice drifted down from the tree.

"Positive. I just can't stop thinking about how the facility threatened to kill him if he left. I mean, I know this whole experiment is a secret…but I didn't know to what extent."

"That's insane," Jared added quietly.

Yet, despite the exciting stories, the mood was darkening with the sky.

"You guys, I'm getting really worried…I'll keep watch next," Lydia offered.

All was silent.

Nodding understandingly, they settled down. Their worries festered in the night, leaving them all on edge. Emily watched with an eagle's eye for the final arrival.

But, before the night could fall over every tree, Mitch moved to whisper to Emily.

"Um…thanks," he said, staring into her face for a second before looking down at his feet. Emily was the only one he felt comfortable talking to; the rest felt like superior beings, and he was just the kid along for the ride.

"For what?" She peered down at him and creased her brows.

"For helping me out yesterday. For forgiving me."

"But you didn't do anything wrong, Mitch." Her eyes seemed to search through his, diving into his brain and sorting through all of his innermost thoughts.

"My mom did, though. I'm so sorry for what she did, Em. I had no idea."

An understanding developed between them.

"Maybe it was better that way," whispered Emily, resting her head against the tree trunk to look at the starry sky. "Sometimes it hurts to know what you can't change. Mitch…thanks. Y'know. For everything."

# CHAPTER TWENTY

Even after Lydia took her spot in the tree to keep watch, Emily couldn't catch a wink of sleep. So many thoughts were tumbling through her mind, and she couldn't quiet them down enough to close her eyes. First off, what was happening to Antonia? Were they hurting her? It terrified Emily to think of what they were capable of. And finally, after some separation from the P.E.I., she needed some time to accept everything they had done to her. After that electrocution experiment, her mind was still constantly on edge. It had been so painful, the electricity pulsing through her body over and over. And Mitch had seen her that way. On the train ride, he'd asked her if she was alright, and although she'd said yes, deep down Emily knew that she would never fully recover from that day. Plus, speaking of Mitch, how had that happened? How had he and she become so friendly in such a short period of time? Something about Mitch made her stomach flutter, and she liked his eyes and his hair and the way he laughed. Emily felt confident that she could trust Mitch…something about him made her believe that he would always make the right choice, always be honest with her. Holding onto that thought, Emily fell into a restless sleep.

# CHAPTER TWENTY-ONE

Lydia sat in the branch of a tree, listening to her friends' breathing slow as they drifted off. Fully alert and wide awake, she peered down the trunk of the tree, watching them sleep soundly. It was so nice to be with them again, to feel at home…well, kind of. She'd never really know where her home was, but in her eyes, it was wherever her fellow Plugs were, however stupid that might sound. Although she'd always hated the P.E.I., seeing her friends after so long made her remember how lonely she'd been in Arizona. A fierce determination filled her, and she was ready to do anything in order to protect her friends.

"Antonia, here we come," she whispered.

# CHAPTER TWENTY-TWO

Mitch kept his eyes shut tight, trying to force himself to fall asleep. Part of him expected to wake up in his bedroom at the facility, his mother glaring at him and ordering him around like always. He wanted to explain to Emily how much he appreciated this; never, ever had he thought that he would actually get out. Emily had done that and much more for him, helping him escape, listening to the things he hadn't been able to share before. So, when his heart wandered back to his mother, twinging with the tiniest inklings of hope, he shivered with guilt. Linda had tortured Emily, again and again.

Mitch rubbed his shoulder where the bullet had nicked him, which still throbbed relentlessly. Bringing his hands to his forehead, he pressed hard against his eyes, wishing he could push away the vision of his mother in the operating room, of his mother having him shot. His stomach churned like it had been thrown in a blender. Although Linda was bitter and stony, Mitch never would have expected her to hurt him…at least physically.

He'd never told his mother about all he knew, all he'd seen; the nights he heard her crying, muttering "James" in her sleep; the mornings he saw her pull a crumpled picture from her pocket, tracing the small faces in the picture with her thumb. These were the images that gave him hope that maybe she was not as terrible as she seemed.

But now, Mitch felt sure that she'd buried any chance of her redemption. Linda had pushed everyone away, and there was only so much a husband or a son could take. Deep down, Mitch longed for his father, the man he'd never met. His heart craved that connection, that sliver of normalcy. Sighing, Mitch turned away from the hope. He knew that his father was long gone, and his insides clenched.

He wished his father had tried a little harder, just for a few more years. He wished he had seen James' face. He wished his father had taught him how to shave, told him about life outside of the facilities, promised that everything would be okay, even if it was a lie.

But most of all, he wished that his dad had stayed because then, Mitch's mom wouldn't have forgotten who she really was.

When his father left, Mitch didn't lose one parent. He lost everything.

# CHAPTER TWENTY-THREE -- ANTONIA

Antonia's skin felt like it was peeling from the bone as the serum spread throughout her body. Her screams ripped her throat raw and tears rushed down her face as the pain worsened tenfold.

The large group of scientists never strayed their eyes from her, pencils at the ready to write down whatever she said.

Her mind was churning out ideas of how to escape the situation, but she discarded most, determining them to be too unlikely. Her vision squirmed violently, muscles spasming as they begged for escape. Yet, through the thick fog of pain, one idea stuck in her mind, and after another three minutes, she decided to go with it, knowing she couldn't last any longer.

Antonia shook her arms and legs violently and then let them go limp. She rolled her head to the side and willed herself to be completely still. The feat was almost impossible with the raging pain. Closing her eyes, she tried to look unconscious, only letting her chest rise and fall the slightest bit with each breath.

A scientist banged on the glass. "Antonia?! Antonia!"

Antonia kept quiet. She listened closely to the voices.

One was shouting. "We need to get her out of there! She's unconscious, she passed out, can't you see?!"

Another clicked on walkie-talkie. "Medical attention needed in Room 005. Now. It's urgent."

The third ordered two guards to open the glass door. "Get her out of there and on the cart, take out the needle!"

The door to Antonia's chamber swung open. Two guards rushed to her side, unlocking the cuffs speedily.

Left hand free. Right leg. Right hand. Left leg.

Antonia felt her body rise into the air. The guards slung her across their arms, laying her on cold metal. One guard left her side, unlocking the main entrance.

Antonia focused on the jingle of keys, waiting for the turn of the door knob. Five seconds…six seconds…

She opened her eyes the tiniest bit. The door was wide open.

The second guard leaned down to observe her face. "I…I think she just woke up." He pressed his thumb to her eyelid and lifted it up, checking for consciousness.

Antonia grabbed his hand and pulled. He toppled forward, hitting his head against the metal cart's edge.

Antonia didn't allow herself to think before she stumbled forward and out the door. Another door to her immediate right lead to a hallway, and jiggling the knob, she ran through, sets of hands grabbing at her from behind. When she finally peeked over her shoulder, she could see scientists and guards alike chasing after her, fury on their faces. She spotted another three guards round the corner ahead, already aiming tranquilizer guns, their snouts pointed at her like wild beasts. By pure instinct, Antonia quickly dropped to the floor, rolling to her right before slamming into the wall besides her. Shouts sounded, bouncing off of the walls and into her ears. Darts springing into the wall above her, she dropped to her stomach and crawled desperately along the floor.

The guards kept their distance, continuing to shoot while circling her. Antonia could feel herself growing tired; the pain was still wearing off. A door at the end of the hallway lead outside of the facility, out to the streets of the city. She was almost there, she had to make it now. Struggling to her feet, Antonia began to run towards the door, shots pinging past her and slipping by her shoulders as blood ran from the needle's place in her arm. She crouched to the floor, running between two of the guards towards the door. Almost there. Almost within reach. Just had to make it to the exit. Her hand gripped the metal knob as she flung the door open.

One last shot pinged from outside the door and sunk into Antonia. Tumbling to the floor at the reaction of the shot, she continued to crawl, hoping to at least get into the city streets before falling asleep from the dart that was nestled in her skin. But, before she could make it any farther, two sets of hands grabbed her feet, while another two pinned down her arms, flipping her onto her back, where she continued to struggle.

"Let go of me! Let go!" screamed Antonia, her whole body shaking with the effort. Kicking her legs out, she managed to make contact with a scientist's chin, but they held firm. She could feel herself slowly drifting away, losing her grasp on reality. "Please...just let me out," she mumbled softly. Her voice sounded completely detached from her body. The fluorescent lights above shone into her eyes, skimming her vision until they blurred into one fuzzy strip of yellow.

# CHAPTER TWENTY-FOUR

The morning sun dipped through the trees. Tensions ran high and a heaviness was beginning to settle over the group. By now, everyone was awake and remembering the events of the previous day. Peering around, the hope that Antonia could have shown up in the middle of the night, safe and smiling, faded quickly. Worried eyes and frowning mouths took over the group until Lydia broke the silence.

"So, Antonia might not be showing up…which means that we need to find her. I say we all pack up and find a train to Albany." Shifting her weight onto her heels and standing up, Lydia motioned for everyone to do the same.

They had to reach Antonia, and fast.

"Do you think she's okay?" Emily asked with uncertainty. Her voice wobbled.

"No, I don't. The quicker we get to Albany, the better."

The group proceeded through Topeka on their way to the train station, heads down, avoiding the eyes of others.

A soft wind moved through the air, the sounds of televisions and cars growing to a dull thrum as the city woke up. It would have been a peaceful scene, had the Plugs not felt desperate to find their friend.

Pausing for a second, Lydia stopped and looked around at the shops. "Wait…we should take what we can to prepare. We don't know what we'll be up against." And with that, she entered the nearest store, one of the few that was open.

Inside, a small TV screen buzzed from where it hung on the wall. A reporter stood in front of a camera. Stopping short, the Plugs stared intently up at the screen.

The reporter began to speak. "It's Maria James here in North Carolina where a break in at a local gas station has occurred. They ask that I do not share the exact location. According to witness Michael Collins, three figures in black suits entered the building and demanded to see security footage. When the shop owner refused, he was, I quote, 'beaten until he allowed them access.' I'll be back with more details in just a minute."

Troy turned to Jared slowly. "It's the guards from my facility. That…that was the gas station I stopped at on my way here."

"I didn't realize it was this serious," Jared shook his head sadly. "I wonder if that man is okay."

Lydia interrupted, stepping in front of the TV screen. "I know it sucks, but we don't have time for that right now. We know that the P.E.I. is panicking, which isn't good for us. We also know that they're willing to hurt people to get us back. They might even be willing to kill. But right now, we just need to focus on finding Antonia. And to do that, we need weapons."

The Plugs moved as a group into an alley behind a row of shops. A few small windows allowed a glimpse into their interiors. In one, a rack of clearance clothing rolled past, pushed by a tall woman with a shiny bob cut. Beside that store sat a butcher's shop. Lydia peered in and spotted a cleaver next to a large slab of meat. Another door led to the front of the shop where a burly man stood hunched over his counter, organizing different cuts of meat into neat rows. Picking up a piece and examining it in his gloved hands, he shook his head and muttered to himself. Suddenly, the door to the back room swung open.

"Get back!" Lydia whispered urgently to her friends, who had stopped behind her. Hurrying behind a massive dumpster, they plugged their noses;

it reeked of rotting animal flesh. Loud footsteps neared their hiding spot, and they held their breath expectantly. Would their journey really end so shortly?

Instead, they heard a bag land in the trash pile with a loud thump. The man was only taking out the garbage. As he headed back inside to grab his second bag, an idea sprouted in Lydia's mind. A butcher shop had knives…even she knew that. Without warning her friends, she jumped up and sprinted in a low crouch to the back door, swinging through it. The back room smelled terrible, and the sight of the bloody flesh made Lydia gag. Scanning the room rapidly, she located a pile of sharp knives and tools that the butcher had only recently been using. Lydia rushed over, grabbed as many as she could, and ran quickly back to the door. As she kicked it open with her foot, a shout sounded behind her. The butcher dropped his bag of trash and hurriedly walked towards her, his hand grazing the collar of her shirt. She accelerated in a flash of panic, running with her friends back to the darkness of the alleyways. As she slowed down, her breathing began to return to normal. Her friends' eyes bore into her.

"Lydia, you could've gotten yourself killed!" Brice reprimanded her. "That wasn't a good idea."

"But, I got us weapons." With that, Lydia let the knives clatter to the ground.

The Plugs gathered them up, tucking them in their pockets.

As they neared the station twenty minutes later, four large figures in the distance appeared, burly men waiting outside of a bar.

"Wonder why they're out so early at the bar…" Troy whispered to Mitch, who jumped back in surprise.

Mitch was completely shocked. Why was a Plug talking to him? He was just a tag along. Somewhere inside of him, he felt his stomach churn when he wondered what they all thought of him.

"Dude, we're not gonna hurt you," laughed Troy. "The only difference between you and me is that I have a chunk of metal inside me."

Mitch nodded. "Yeah, I guess." His floppy hair fell over his eye and he pushed it away, staring down at the pavement.

Lydia was the first to move closer to the group of men, but none of them noticed her, continuing to stumble around. They were clearly drunk and must have been at the bar all night. Every few minutes, a maniacal laugh erupted from one of their throats.

In a store next to the bar, TV screens flashed. But it wasn't another energy crisis report that played across the screen. It was the face of every Plug except for Antonia, and each was being described in great detail. Emily stopped and stooped to watch the report in the store window. The door was open, and noise poured onto the streets. Their names were slowly read off of a list; "Troy, Brice, Lydia…" the voice droned on. Emily's image appeared on the screen.

"Wait, do I really have a zit there?!" Emily flung her hand to her face.

Shushing her, Lydia grabbed her hand and dragged her away from the television.

"Let's just be quiet and subtle," Jared whispered as they began to pass the four men. "They're probably too drunk to notice us."

Lydia could feel the panic rising in her chest. She had forgotten to tell the others about the fact that the facilities had been broadcasting their disappearance all over the country since their escape, and now they were figuring out the hard way. As she backed up slowly, she whispered over her shoulder, "Start running. I forgot to tell you. We've been on TV for days."

"For days?!" Jared whisper-shouted. "This isn't the first report?!"

The group stepped slowly away from the men, steadying their breaths.

"We need to find a way to dis—" Emily murmured before being interrupted.

"Hey, you're those people! From the news!" One of the more sober men stood up, motioning for his friends to do the same. Soon, the four were standing just a few feet from the Plugs.

"RUN!" Lydia screamed. She began sprinting, the rest of the group right behind her.

"Where are we going?" Emily shouted to the others.

"I don't know. Just follow me!"

# CHAPTER TWENTY-FIVE

"Not trying to break your focus, Lydia, but where are we going?" Jared breathed steadily. All of their training at the facility was finally paying off for them and working against the P.E.I. The footsteps of the men were fading away.

Turning sharply down an alleyway, the group stooped down and leaned against the wall, heads in their hands. Emily was the first to break the silence.

"We were on TV?" Her eyes fell upon Lydia, who was staring upwards with her hands resting below her bent knees.

She stared straight at Emily and responded, "Yeah…and whoever finds us is getting a pretty huge reward." Heavy sighs filled the air, hope seeping out of the group's spirit.

"How could we do this? We escape to find each other, but what are we going to do now? We can't live normal lives—not now, not ever—with everyone searching for us," Emily hissed tensely.

"I know…let's just get to the Albany facility. Antonia's definitely in trouble if she hasn't shown up by now," Troy demanded. A sinking feeling dropped into his stomach like an anchor as he realized that something truly must be wrong. Why wouldn't Antonia be there otherwise?

"I agree." Mitch was finally speaking up, slowly growing more confident. "No one on the streets will recognize me. Let me go check if the coast is clear."

"Fine. But go quickly. We can't just sit here, they'll find us," quipped Brice, panting heavily and pointing down the alleyway.

Before Mitch could fully exit, Emily shot up and trapped his forearm, quickly letting go in shock at herself. "Just...be careful," she whispered. He nodded silently and left. The group sat, waiting for his return and for answers.

"What do you think's going to happen?" Emily asked tensely.

"I don't know. I really don't. But I'm not gonna let them separate us again. You guys are all I have," Troy said slowly, shaking his head as if realizing just how dire their situation was. His hands were twitching as he continued glancing down the alley every few seconds to check for Mitch.

"Me neither. If I lose you guys...I don't know what I'll do.' Lydia stood up. Slowly, she began handing out the knives she'd taken from the butcher shop.

"You're right,' Emily stated firmly, shooting up to take a weapon from Lydia. "We're not going down without a fight. They can't control us anymore. And they can't take you all away from me again." Her nostrils flared, and it was the angriest anyone had ever seen Emily. She seemed more determined than ever as she strode steadily back and forth.

Minutes felt like hours as they waited for Mitch to return, hopefully with some information that could help them. Emily felt on edge as she drummed her fingers against the side of her thigh impatiently.

Suddenly, a loud yell sounded from far away, but became muffled quickly like someone screaming underwater. Brice stood up, slowly approaching the alleyway entrance. "I don't know what that was...but it didn't sound good."

Emily also rose to her feet, walked to the entrance, and poked her head out cautiously. "What if that was him? I'm going out to look." Before she could fully leave, the rest of the Plugs were surrounding her, blocking her exit.

"Emily, you can't do this." Lydia's voice shook for the first time since their initial reunion.

"Please, don't, we don't know what's out there." Jared was holding Emily's wrist, and a look of pleading entered his eyes.

"Yeah, what if they get you too?" Peering back and forth down the empty street, Troy looked at his friends and blinked slowly. "Let's all go. I'm not letting anyone leave this alley alone." His voice had a tone of definitiveness to it, and the group nodded sharply, preparing their knives in their hands.

One by one, Lydia, then Brice and Jared, and finally Emily and Troy exited the abandoned alleyway, clutching their weapons tightly.

"Where'd the yell come from?" whispered Emily. Brice pointed down the sidewalk, and the five of them moved simultaneously as a pack. As they crept, Lydia suddenly shot out her arm and held her finger to her lips, silently warning the group to stay quiet.

"Wait. I hear something." Her voice was barely audible, but it was enough to bring them all to a stop. Whipping around quickly, Troy gasped and backed away, bringing the rest of the pack along behind his outstretched arm.

"Nice to see you all again," Linda grinned. Behind her, three guards were gathered, two holding a boy tightly in their arms at gunpoint: Mitch.

# CHAPTER TWENTY-SIX

"Let go of him," Emily snarled, pushing through Troy's arm and stepping closer to Linda. "Let go of him now." There was a tremor to her voice, a threat lurking in the depths of her sharp tone. Her hand was buried deep in her pocket as she reached for her knife, ready to use it against Linda if that was what it took. Realizing this was going to be a fight, Jared, Brice, Lydia, and Troy lined up next to her, pulling their weapons out of their pockets and holding them to their sides.

"If you so much as touch one of us, including Mitch, I'll use this knife, I swear." Lydia had her right hand raised, the handle of the knife gripped tightly in her palm. She seemed ready to take desperate measures, and as if on cue, the rest of the group revealed their weapons, raising them so that the sunlight glinted off of them.

"We won't hurt him...on one condition. You all," Linda pointed to each Plug slowly, "come with us. Simple deal." She motioned to the guards around her. The two holding Mitch nodded menacingly. The trigger of their guns clicked loudly, and in a flurry of motion, Lydia lunged at Linda's thigh, burying the knife deep in her flesh.

Blood splattered onto the pavement as Linda moaned and curled into a ball to examine her injured leg. In the commotion, the two guards holding Mitch loosened their grip in surprise just enough for him to escape. He fell to the ground loudly and scrambled backwards towards the Plugs, staring in horror at his writhing mother. The three guards raised their guns threateningly, but they knew they couldn't actually kill any of the teens except for Mitch. Stepping forward, they each cocked their pistols, aiming at the Plugs' feet and legs. It seemed like they had been given both real guns and tranquilizer guns for the occasion. The Plugs surged forward, and following Lydia's lead, they stampeded towards the pack of guards, weapons held high. Bullets ricocheted off of the concrete as Emily danced her way across, lunging forward as her knife became embedded in the shoulder of a guard. Dropping his gun, he backed away, staring down at his shoulder with a shocked expression. Before he could react, Emily gripped his gun and started firing bullets into the legs of the guards. Brice ran behind the guards, tackling them as Emily shot at their thighs. Desperate to help, Jared and Troy sprinted to pick up stray bricks on the side of the road and used them to swipe at the fallen guards, rendering them unconscious. The Plugs were surprised, confused at how they could fight. It dawned on them that if this were anyone else attacking them, they probably wouldn't have fared so well, but because it was the people who had ruined their lives, their fury made for a strong weapon. They were finally thankful for the intense fitness regimens they had been forced to follow at the facilities. The guards were weakening, unable to move, and moaning as they tried to examine their wounds.

Lydia began to sprint, the rest of the group, including Mitch, close behind. When they finally reached a spot that was far enough away, they all slouched to the ground, panting heavily to catch their breath. Troy was holding his side and squeezing his eyes shut, Emily and Lydia staring into the air in shock, and Brice twirling a gun in his hands slowly, a tired look in his eyes. Mitch sat stiffly, eyes wide open and body tense, never having experienced anything like that before.

But, Jared was still standing up, pacing back and forth excitedly with a smile on his face. "Oh, we're good."

Ignoring him, Lydia gripped her knife tighter. "We need to go. They know where we are, and they know that we're going to try to help Antonia."

"At least we've got guns, now," Emily breathed, brandishing her new weapon.

The group rushed through the city, distancing themselves from Linda and the guards. Every second weighed heavily upon their shoulders; there was no time to waste.

The train station loomed in the distance, it's metal walls glimmering under a bright sun. The only noise that could be heard was the squealing of trains on the tracks, and far, far off, the sound of a horn blaring. It was decided that Mitch would do the talking, since he was the least known fugitive; his face hadn't been broadcast on the news yet.

Mitch wrung his hands. "What if they recognize me? Maybe my face is on the news now, after that fight. We could be walking right into a trap, you guys."

"I don't think you became the headline news story in the thirty minutes since we fought the guards," Jared offered.

"We don't have a choice, anyways. Let's just get a move on." Brice gestured towards the doors of the station.

Lydia rolled her eyes, elbowing Mitch and shushing Brice. "No one will suspect anything, so long as you keep it together, Mitch. No pressure...actually, that's a lie. You can't mess this up."

# CHAPTER TWENTY-SEVEN -- ANTONIA

Now fully awake, Antonia was becoming more and more aware of the facility's plan. She listened intently to whispers and pretended to sleep as the scientists spoke. To her relief, the Plugs had survived the first stage of the P.E.I.'s attempts to find and capture them. The facility was going to increase the reach and frequency of their broadcasts. They would offer immeasurable rewards to whoever found the Plugs first. And they knew that the Plugs were coming to find her, somehow. Soon, they'd be headed right into the facility's trap, thinking they were saving Antonia, but really handing themselves over.

Still wrenching her wrists against the metal cuffs restraining them, she could only wait and watch the disaster play out.

# CHAPTER TWENTY-EIGHT

"Okay, don't talk, keep your heads down" Lydia whispered outside the station door.

If they were careful, they might just have a chance at actually getting through the trip without being recognized. A rush of cool air flooded through the wide doors as Lydia swung them open and walked into the station, closely followed by the rest of the group. As they neared the row of ticket desks, a short woman glared up at them with narrowed and beady eyes, visibly pressing her chewing gum onto the roof of her mouth.

"Uh…hi…six tickets, please…" muttered Mitch, wide eyes staring straight at the woman. His hands twitched slightly as he laid the money down on the table.

Thinking to herself, Emily tried to figure out how much Mitch had contributed. It certainly was a lot, and she was grateful that he'd taken cash from Linda. As she glanced his way, she noticed him clenching his fists under the counter. Emily had seen him do this a few times before, when something was bothering him. She especially remembered him doing this when he first told her about his relation to Linda.

"What's wrong with him?" Jared whispered into Emily's ear, creasing his brows and folding his arms.

Troy was standing next to him, tapping his foot. Quietly, he turned to Emily and asked, "Yeah, do you know what's up with him? Why's he all…shaky?"

For the first time, a croaking voice emerged from the woman. "That'll be enough for 'em. Train boards in one hour."

With that, she slapped six tickets into Mitch's open palm, retrieved the gum from the roof of her mouth, and proceeded to chew.

The waiting area for their train was mostly empty except for a few people with headphones. It was a quiet walk from the ticket desk, everyone following Lydia's advice to stay silent and unnoticed. The six of them sat down in benches opposite each other, staring out at the empty track and waiting for the train.

Surprising everyone, Mitch was the first to speak, but he kept his voice low all the same, a hushed whisper that carried across the space between the seats. "I'm, uh, just gonna run to the bathroom, be back in a second," he declared abruptly, standing up and turning away. His hand slipped into his pocket and stayed there, and as he trudged away, Emily held up a finger to Lydia and hurried over to him nervously.

"Hey, you seem…off. What's up?" She grabbed Mitch's hand to stop him, and they simultaneously peered down at their hands touching, letting go quickly and taking a step away from each other. "Sorry…I just, um…yeah." She laughed, an awkward feeling growing between them as she lifted her eyes to him again. "Really, though…is there anything you want to tell me?"

Mitch met her eyes. "Yeah, I'm fine, just noticing how, uh, pretty you look today," he said.

But to Emily, his voice sounded hollow, and it just worried her more.

"That kind of came out of nowhere, but, thanks." She was about to turn away, brushing her hair behind her ears, but she spun on her heels and tilted her head, a confused look appearing on her face. "Is there something…between us? I can't handle any more questions in my life, so if there is, just say it."

Mitch's answer sounded so artificial, her heart plunged quickly.

"Yeah, Em, I…uh…really like you," he nodded. And with that, he entered the bathroom.

Emily trudged back to her seat and let herself fall into it. Biting her nails one by one, she watched the bathroom door like it might catch on fire at any second.

Troy tapped her elbow, pulling her out of her trance.

"Emily, can I talk to you for a second?" His jaw was clenched.

"What?" Her eyes were still distracted.

"We need to talk."

"Yeah, of course."

The two moved to the opposite side of the room, away from the bathroom and the group.

Troy let his thoughts burst out of him like he was gasping for oxygen. "I don't trust him."

"Who?"

"Mitch. I just…okay, don't hate me. Please?"

"I would never hate you, Troy. You know that."

"I'm really good at reading people, Emily. And I get this awful…this weird vibe from Mitch. He's not telling us everything. He's holding something back, I swear."

"Why would you think that?"

"It's something about his eyes. It's like he won't look at you right. Like he's guilty, but…determined? I don't know. But something's not right here."

"I'm not mad, Troy, but I think you're wrong. I wouldn't be here without Mitch."

"I care about you way too much to not tell you what I believe, and I really don't want you to get hurt, Em. Please, please be careful. Watch closely."

Emily rolled her eyes.

"Do you promise me?"

"I promise."

"Thank you." Troy sighed in relief.

"God, why are you acting like my older brother."

A smirk crossed his face. "What can I say? You're my nonbiological sister. Just trust me on this one."

"Fine. I'll watch, but nothing is gonna happen. I know Mitch. He wouldn't hurt me."

"You can't be totally sure of that, though."

# CHAPTER TWENTY-NINE

"Okay, let's go," whispered Lydia.

An announcement had just been made that their train was boarding. People in the surrounding seats stood, wheeling their suitcases behind them as they stepped onto the platform and into the stuffy train. Lydia could smell hand sanitizer and sweat.

Once they finally boarded the train and settled in, with Brice sitting alone, Jared, Emily, and Mitch sitting together, and Lydia and Troy directly in front of them, Mitch began to speak in hushed tones.

"I know you probably don't want to talk about it, but what did they do to you guys at the facility? I can't be left in the dark this entire time." It was the first time Mitch had talked since explaining who he was to everyone. A hint of desperation could be found in his voice, and Emily's heart ached for a moment, sad for the boy who knew nothing about his so-called home. He stared around the group expectantly, waiting for an answer. It took a minute, but finally Lydia spoke up.

"Do you really want to know, Mitch?" She seemed tired, like the terrible memories were too much to take on top of Antonia's absence.

"Yeah. I mean, yes. Yes, I want to know." His fingers twitched impatiently as he bit his lip and stared.

"I don't know if they did the same exact things to all of us, but I'm sure it's pretty similar." Lydia took on a monotone voice, clearly attempting to disconnect herself with the experiences. Her pulse was already speeding up, as if she would need to start running from the scientists any minute. But she was able to slow it down enough to speak. "Well, I'll give you the backdrop first. We're called Plugs. That's because we have these little sensors that plug into our shoulders. It's kind of hard to explain, but it all relates back to piezoelectricity. Something in our DNA allows us to harness more energy, and all of that is transferred through our sensors and made into electric energy. But, we can't live without our sensors, because the scientist needed to attach them to some vital arteries. The removal of the plugs would rupture them. I know, great idea, huh?"

Mitch nodded, seeming a bit confused but still following. "Well, not a good idea, bu—"

Lydia interrupted. She clearly wanted to get the conversation over with. "Okay, good. If we are successful—not we, but the scientists, I should say—in the mission, then the United States won't need to rely on other countries anymore, because we provide a good portion of energy. The scientists can store all of that energy we produce in machines, so even though we're gone, I'd say they have about a week or two worth of energy stored up. So, if we're out for more than two weeks, that's when they're really screwed." She paused, smiling a little to herself. "We were made for convenience, kind of. Our lives were sacrificed for the country's comfort, everyone's reliance on electricity and growing demands for fossil fuels, basically. No one likes depending on other countries for resources. No one likes dirty power plants. So, here we are. But that's not what you asked. We had to do a ton of stuff to keep our energy supply balanced. We were taken away from our families, not allowed any friends. No contact with the outside world. No childhood experiences. Our lives and love were taken from us. We had to do certain exercises for a certain amount of time, eat certain foods, all of those stupid things. Oh, and we can't forget, we also got tested all the time to determine how much energy we can supply in certain situations and if we can still produce energy during certain...catastrophes."

Shuddering, Mitch closed his eyes briefly, remembering the terrible test he observed Emily go through. His heart began to pound louder, louder, until he could feel it in his fingertips and hear it in his ears.

Lydia sighed. "You guys should try to get some rest. I'll take first watch." She turned back around in her seat.

Too many thoughts were running through Troy's mind, and the idea of sleep seemed unachievable. With Lydia on lookout, he allowed himself to speak what he'd been feeling since leaving the facility. "Don't you feel guilty? I just feel like, if we were at our facilities, no one would be panicking. The guards wouldn't be beating people up to find us. What if the guards start hurting the scientists there? What if they think that some of the scientists have information? Maybe we need to go back, make them promise to change if we return."

"I don't think us supplying the world with energy is any better than letting everyone panic. Actually, I think it's much worse. Think about it. Maybe they'll research us more and try to make more people like us. Maybe us leaving will help them gain some of their humanity back. Because Troy, if our success is worth more than the lives of all the scientists at the facility, and if energy is worth taking away the lives of six babies, then the world sure has lost a lot of its humanity. They didn't give us any choice. Our lives were set for us before we could even walk."

"I know, Lydia. I agree. And the fact that people were willing to ruin our lives because they were so desperately greedy for an energy solution is scary too. I don't know how we're gonna fix this all, but I do know that we can't let them hurt more people like they hurt us!"

"You're right. We can't." Allowing her head to fall back against the soft head rest of the chair, she felt the pressure and fear start to consume her. Lydia wondered if they should've never left their facilities in the first place. Although they were free, they were also lost; no shelter, no plan, no hiding. But, deciding to focus solely on saving Antonia, she buried the thought in the back of her mind.

# CHAPTER THIRTY

Jared was awakened by an old woman with white hair and a camo shirt. Her wrinkled forehead was so close to his, that when he first opened his eyes, he shot up in his seat and kicked out his legs frantically.

"Hey, boy, I know you," whispered the woman, leaning into Jared's ear. "And don't try to fool me. I haven't lost my mind just yet."

Beckoning to the restroom area down the aisle, she began to walk over, purse swinging on her arm as her feet rustled against the thinly carpeted floor. Not to his surprise, Lydia had managed to stay awake, and she swung around rapidly in her seat. "Deny everything," she whisper-shouted, "unless she proves herself to be helpful."

After a curt nod, Jared pushed himself to his feet and retreated anxiously to the rear of the train. A mighty sunset outside the window distracted him for a moment. The pinks, blues, and greens scattered against the green plains reminded him of a painting, and of another reason why they needed to escape: to see things like this; to see the beauty left in the world, without a window between them. A hiss erupted from the old woman, which he deciphered as, "Hurry up, boy!"

Snapping out of his trance and ripping his glance away from the sunset, he walked down the aisle at a quick pace, slowing as he neared the woman.

"Don't talk. I know who you are, you're one of them Plugs" She spat the word "Plugs" as if it felt dirty on her lips and looked up towards him once again. "I've heard about you, secrets being passed around…but I didn't know for sure that you were real. God, I hoped you weren't. But you need to understand something…most people out there…they're starving. And I don't mean for food, I mean for energy. They're starving when they shouldn't be, and I think they ought to keep starving until they realize just how damn full their stomachs really are. The government is already working to find more oil, and they're getting desperate. But you can't let them think that your human life has less value than their rotten cars and televisions! And damn it, they don't!"

Taken aback, Jared opened his mouth and closed it twice before blurting out a question that reigned in his mind. "So, are you for or against…us?"

"I'm against the P.E.I. Against you? Now, that depends. When I was a young adult like you…we saw this coming. Only a few of us were smart enough to open our mouths and say it, and before long, we've got an energy crisis on our hands, for God's sake!"

"And…why are you telling me all this?"

"To warn you. To be the last person who opens their mouth while they still can. You can't go back to the facilities."

"Who are you?" said Jared.

"Jane Simmal. And there are others like me. There are others who want to fight." With that, she slipped him a small piece of paper and turned around to leave.

Jared called her name, unable to stop himself. He hesitated. "Jane…if you know about us, then…do you know where the facilities are?"

She moved back towards Jared. "I only know of one facility."

"Where?"

"And I only know what I've heard through rumors."

"You need to tell me where you think it is."

"Are you trying to go back?"

Jared looked behind him at Lydia. He knew he was telling Jane too much, but this might be the Plugs' best chance of finding Antonia. "No, but there's something there that we want."

Jane chewed on her lip, deciding whether she believed him. Finally, she spoke. "I've been told that it's on the east side of the city…in a white building. Somewhere near a pawn shop named the Horvett." With that, she stalked away.

Jared eyed the paper warily, unsure what it might say. Letting his eyes graze the sloppy writing, he deciphered an address he could only assume belonged to her home. He returned to his seat more shaken up than ever…more, even, than how he'd felt during all of the tests he had gone through. A terrible feeling of knowing, of being aware of something that he didn't really want to be aware of, was creeping through him.

Suddenly, the sunset outside didn't seem as beautiful; sleep seemed further away than Antonia; and a normal life, an undiscovered galaxy.

Lydia had been watching from afar, and when he returned looking sullen, she whipped around in her seat. "What'd she say? What happened?"

Unable to speak, Jared swallowed loudly, a frown crossing his usually bright face.

"Are you alright?" Lydia reached out to put her hand on his shoulder, waving her other hand in front of his eyes. "You're seriously starting to freak me out…"

Although it took a few minutes, he was finally able to gain his composure, and he swallowed again before telling her everything that happened.

"She…she said that she heard about us, but thought we were only a rumor. And she thinks that it's wrong to take away people's lives for energy. She seemed really passionate about it, like she really cared."

A grimace appeared on Lydia's face. "Jared…I…" she hesitated, "just don't know. There's too much going on right now. I, I can't think clearly! We've got to find Antonia, stay away from practically everyone, and then figure out what to do with our lives!" She widened her eyes and lowered her voice in horror, finally expressing her deepest concern. "Even if we do save Antonia…" her breath caught. "They'll never stop looking for us; never stop hunting us down."

For the first time, Jared saw a flicker of panic behind Lydia's eyes. Lydia, the collected one, the problem-solver, the leader, was showing fear and indecision. She seemed afraid to show any vulnerability, even to herself…but this time she could not contain it.

"Lydia, relax. We know that you're strong and all, but we've also known you since you were born. It's alright to break down a little bit."

A tear fell from her eye and she wiped it away quickly, sniffling loudly and breathing deeply as if to cleanse herself of the emotions she was feeling. Nodding, she managed to smile at Jared before turning to face forward again. Her hands were shaking slightly, and to calm them she grabbed a napkin from her pocket. The napkin swiveled through her fingers quickly, in and out, in and out, in a hypnotic fashion.

Leaning forward, Jared tapped Lydia on the shoulder lightly. "Hey, go to sleep. I'll take watch."

Hesitating a moment, she finally gave in, a visible slump in her form when she turned back around in her seat. Jared had only seen her show her exhaustion, her pain, a few times before, and it reminded him that being a leader was not easy.

Meanwhile, Brice was staring into the silky blackness outside with thoughts tumbling through his mind. The full extent of their problems was beginning to truly sink in, sending weariness through him. Sure, they had escaped, but what now? Plastic surgery to mask their identity? Continue to live on the run? How would they ever live a free life? Someone was bound to question them, to find them eventually. And Antonia, who hadn't been able to escape, was probably being put through hell in the P.E.I.'s attempts to find them. All of this information fell on him like a dead weight until his life felt like a puzzle with too many missing pieces. He had sat alone, feeling like he needed to sort through his thoughts, come up with a rough plan of what lay ahead of him. But his mind was overloaded, making his efforts useless, and his ideas only reminded him of the terrible days at the facility.

# CHAPTER THIRTY-ONE

"I seriously didn't think we'd get through that ride without being recognized," Emily admitted once they were outside the station. It was 11:37 P.M.

"Well, we actually did get recognized," Lydia interjected, stepping into the center of the small circle they'd made and informing them of the incident on the train ride. "A woman named Jane approached Jared and told him that she had heard all about us. She mentioned the energy crisis. But unlike the scientists, she said that we don't deserve this, and that we can't encourage the creation of more Plugs by returning to the facilities."

The Plugs, in addition to Mitch, stared with wide eyes. For the first time, they felt guilty for doing what they were supposed to be doing, for producing electricity. They were quiet for a long while, staring into space with saddened eyes and crossed arms.

Lydia tried her best to hold back any signs of fear. "I know this is a lot of pressure, but we need to focus on saving Antonia first. Then, we can decide whether to stay out here…or go back." She paused for a moment, debating whether or not she should say what hovered in her mind. "But, I don't think we should go back. It's not right for anyone…" Lydia gazed at her feet solemnly. "So, let's get going."

The group hurried to a hidden spot behind the train station, praying that they wouldn't be seen. They crept along, jumping at every noise and making sure only to speak when necessary. An eerie feeling settled over them now. Although they knew the danger of their plan, they also knew that saving their friend was more important than anything else. No matter what happened, they needed to at least try for Antonia's sake.

Although Lydia was reluctant to stop for rest, she knew that the group would need energy if they were going to fight off the facility's guards. "We've got to take a break," she said suddenly, slumping against the brick wall.

Emily yawned loudly in agreement. "Any ideas where to sleep?"

"We can't just stop," Brice argued in exasperation. "The timing gives us the element of surprise!"

"Our element of surprise won't matter if we can't throw a punch," Jared sighed. "The station isn't boarding any passengers now, and that was the last stop of the night, so let's just stay here for a while."

"I'll take first watch," Lydia murmured. "Who wants to join?"

"I'll help." Emily walked over to Lydia's side.

"Do you really think this is the best idea?" Brice crossed his arms.

"I, personally, would rather not pass out while trying to shoot a gun." Closing his eyes, Jared let out a lengthy sigh. "I'm exhausted."

"Fine," Brice huffed. "But you all need to study up on surprise attacks, okay?"

"We're a little preoccupied right now I think, Brice. But thanks for the suggestion," Lydia teased, shoving him lightly on the shoulder.

Shrugging, the boys muttered their thanks and sat against the cold brick, letting their heads loll back. Soon, they were snoring.

Emily and Lydia sat side by side, their shoulders touching. They didn't speak, just breathed slowly, deliberately, willing their minds to keep calm and clear.

"It's so weird," Emily whispered in awe.

"What?" Automatically assuming the worst, Lydia turned to her friend with sharp eyes.

But Emily didn't see this. She lay back on the concrete, pointing at the stars that had emerged during the night. "This," she laughed, as if it all were inexplicably obvious. "That a few nights ago, we were all in different states, waiting for this moment," she elaborated, letting her arm drop beside her. "I've always wanted this. I mean…not the cold ground and the rescue missions. But the freedom." She looked around her, at her friends scattered along the ground. "And now that I have it, I know I can't go back. It would just hurt too much."

\*\*\*

"It's going to be really hard to find this place," Brice admitted. "And it's not like we can go asking people for directions. They probably don't even know where or what the facility is."

"Wait, wait." Jared gulped. "Okay, don't kill me, but that lady I met on the train…I asked her where the facility was."

"Jared!" Lydia glared at him. "We don't know if we can trust her."

"Did you have a better idea to find Antonia?"

"Not exactly…but that was way too risky."

"Whatever!" Jared threw his hands in the air. "At least we can find her faster. The lady said it was in the eastern part of Albany, and it was a white building, near a pawn shop called the Horvett. That's all she told me."

"Fine. But, before we attack, we actually need a game plan. We can't just storm the place." Lydia pointed out.

"So, what do we do?" asked Emily.

Brice rubbed his hands together. "I have an idea…Mitch, do you have any more money?"

"Yeah, a little. Why?"

"We're gonna need you to do some shopping for us."

An hour later, after Mitch had checked the yellow pages for the Horvett and purchased the baseball bats and fireworks that Lydia had requested, the Plugs snuck through the city, peering around every corner. They darted through alleys, ducked under windows, and sprinted across streets.

Jared scoured the streets for the pawn shop, pointing excitedly when he spotted a "Horvett" sign on a squat building.

By the time the city was fully waking up, they stood a few blocks away from the facility, conversing fervently.

Lydia began to whisper. "Does everyone have their weapons?" Knives emerged from pockets, and Lydia gripped hers tightly as her knuckles turned white. Brice and Emily had managed to hold onto their guns from the encounter with Linda back in Topeka. They brandished them now. "Okay, then. I think we're ready."

Motioning with his hand, Brice turned on his heel and shuffled towards the front of the small building they hid behind. Before he could reach the street beyond, Mitch yelled, "Wait!"

To their surprise, he tensely volunteered to stay behind. Jared met eyes with Emily, a questioning look on his face. Mitch had been acting weird lately, and of all people, they expected Emily to know what was wrong. But it was obvious that she had absolutely no clue. When they turned to leave the alleyway again, Jared shouted to stop and stared towards the ground meekly.

"Uh, I know we haven't lost yet. And I know that we've only gotten to be together for a little bit. But, if we do end up getting caught…" He shifted his gaze to them and lifted a corner of his mouth in an attempt at a grin. "We'll…we'll be fine, but I'm just saying, if we aren't…you guys are my family, my brothers and sisters. And I feel honored and glad to have loved you all."

***

Crouched outside of the facility, the Plugs murmured in hushed tones.

"So, how do we actually find her?" Emily looked over towards the facility and back to the Plugs, a distinctive glimmer in her eyes.

"Well…we know that our facilities had the same rooms. Maybe they had the same layout, too." Lydia's face lit up at the thought. "That could help us know where we're going…know what to avoid, know where to find her. Ummm, let's see. My bedroom was in the East Wing, third door down," she said hopefully.

Thinking back to their own rooms, the Plugs nodded in agreement.

"What if that's the only similarity?" Jared worried aloud. "The North Wing in my facility was the scary one, the one with all the testing labs and the operating rooms."

"Mine too," Emily said excitedly.

The rest of the Plugs murmured their assent as well.

"Then that's it," Lydia decided. "I'm sure they're keeping her somewhere in the North Wing, as punishment."

"Yeah, but how're we going to find which room she's in?" Brice pointed out tensely.

"We listen for her voice. Or her screams," Lydia said bravely, staring at the door to the facility and swallowing loudly.

# CHAPTER THIRTY-TWO

As the group neared the doors, they exchanged glances of apprehension. There appeared to be a mutual agreement that they would stay quiet. They sprinted along the side of the building, finding a side door.

Although it seemed unlikely that the entrance would be unlocked, they nodded towards Troy, who was closest to it. Reaching out a slightly shaking hand, he gripped the cool metal of the doorknob and turned it slowly, listening for an alarm. When none sounded, he turned around to face the Plugs and raised his brows in question as to whether they should enter. Although suspicious, they slipped through the door. The first to enter the building, Troy was hit with a fresh wave of sterilizing solution and bleach. The experience felt almost creepy in a way, like he was back at an old jail cell, peering from the outside in. As far as he could see, the hallways were empty. Troy gestured to the others that it was all right to pass, holding the door for Jared and crouching down as soon as he took the door. The rest did the same until all five of them stood huddled next to the door, bodies pressed against the wall. Looking towards the right hallway, Emily spotted a cafeteria, empty with the lights out. Bedrooms lined the hallways, but no one was inside. The whole place was...deserted. She nodded her head to the left, and they all stood as a unit, running in a crouched position down the hallway until another turn was reached. Lydia looked at each of them and held up her weapon, signaling that if there was going to be a fight, it would be soon. With that, she ran towards the two metal doors to the operating room. Cold air was seeping out from under the cracks in the door, and all was silent for a few seconds, until muffled shouts could be heard from inside the room. "Don' d' i', stay ou'!"

A horrified look passed over Brice's face and he locked eyes with Lydia rigidly. He voiced the question that had first come to all of their heads when they heard the terrified voice. "Is that Antonia?!"

Lydia returned a solemn nod to Brice. "Get in your positions," she mouthed.

Lydia and Brice moved twenty feet down the hallway, pulling out a firework and a lighter. They aimed the firework directly at the ceiling. Jared and Emily held their bats behind their heads, crouched out of sight, ready to swing. Troy stood right outside the operating room's doors, gun in hand.

Lydia raised a hand, all five of her fingers held up rigidly. One finger went down, the tip at her palm. The second finger went down. Now, there were only three left, two left. And finally, one.

When the last finger met her palm, Brice flicked on the lighter, setting fire to the wick of the firework. Lydia and he sprinted down the hall. The flame crept down the wick until it finally set the firework off, a whining noise exploding into the room. The gold firework shot up, twirling in the air until it hit the ceiling. The first explosion went off, gold and red sparkles littering the hallway. Smaller explosions stemmed off of the main firework, off one by one, boom after boom, smoke spreading into every nook and cranny. Ashes floating to the ground, the entire hallway filled with a hazy fog.

The fire alarm started to blare, its shrill scream breaking through the crackles of the fireworks, and a moment later, the small shower heads along the hallway drenched the floor with water.

The door to the operating room slammed open, two guards rushing out in a panic. They stumbled through the smoke, slipping along the wet floor.

"Hey! We know you're here!" one of them bellowed. "We can do this the easy way, or the hard way!"

The Plugs held their breath, waiting for the perfect moment to strike.

The ceiling started to crumble, pieces breaking off and falling to the ground. As the guards rushed towards the source of damage, scanning the hall for the Plugs, Emily and Jared ran behind them. They swung in perfect synchronization, delivering audible cracks to the guards' heads.

The guards sagged to the ground.

As they did so, Troy ran into the operating room, holding his gun out in front of him. It suddenly became obvious to him that there was a reason the door was left unlocked, a reason it had been so simple to make it into the facility: the scientists had wanted them to. Linda and two more guards stood over Antonia. Her mouth was gagged, hands and feet strapped together.

Before anyone had the chance to whisper a word, Troy whipped out his gun. At that moment, Brice, Lydia, Emily, and Jared returned from the hall, soaking wet.

Lydia and Brice were covered in soot and still coughing, but they pulled out their weapons without hesitation.

The room was silent for a moment, the Plugs staring at the guards and Linda.

Linda stayed over Antonia, hand tight on her shoulder. Her eyes bulged, mouth open in shock. "You can't keep hiding," she hissed. "You belong to us!"

As she stepped forward, Troy broke out of his stupor. Aiming at the nearest guard, he pulled the trigger and nailed him in the shoulder.

Weapons swung and punches flew through the air as the room became a frenzy of movement.

Managing to grab the tranquilizer gun from the guard Troy had taken down, Lydia started to shoot at the two people in the back of the room, starting with Linda. The guard dodged her bullet and slipped out of her line of fire, but she hit Linda in the leg and watched her fall with a sense of triumph.

As Linda lost consciousness, the guard that Troy had shot in the shoulder regained enough strength to stand.

He lunged at Troy, the other guard going for Jared, and Lydia realized that they had been given permission to hurt the Plugs. As the four fell to to the ground in a jumble of flying limbs, Jared's arm swung out and collided with Emily's face; her nose started to gush with blood. Troy and Jared squirmed out from underneath the guards and cleared out of the way frantically, allowing Lydia a clear shot. Before she could take it, one of the guards flipped onto his back and shot, a tranquilizer dart plunging straight into Lydia's leg. Looking down in shock for a moment, she ripped it out and swung her fist back, connecting with the man's face. He held his jaw, face crumpling in pain. Then, Lydia shot him with a dart for good measure.

A hazy shadow passed over Lydia's eyes as the effects of the tranquilizer set in. The ceiling seemed to swap places with the floor, and the guards swung in and out of her vision. Suddenly, she fell to her knees, hands pressed against the ground so that she was on all fours. The rest of the group gathered around her, shaking her in an attempt to keep her awake, but their actions were fruitless. Her body slumped with sleep, and they stood up, exchanging momentary glances of the panic they all felt.

Brice cut away the final strap, gripping Antonia's upper arm and pulling her to her feet. He immediately handed some of the straps she had been held with to her while keeping some for himself and knelt beside the unconscious guards. They bound arms and legs tightly together, and once they were done, they stood up, surveying the individual battles left around them.

"Antonia, I'd love to give you a warm welcome, but I think that'll have to wait," panted Jared, his chest heaving as he gained back his breath.

Brice and Emily rushed back to Lydia and dragged her up from the floor, slinging her arms over their shoulders. They both sagged under the dead weight but nodded when Antonia asked if they were ready. The hallway still seemed to be empty, and they wondered if the rest of the scientists had been sent away. They remained cautious. The alarm's noisy ring echoed down the hallway, reverberating off of the walls and bouncing back into the Plugs' ears. Taking a brief look around, Emily noticed some minor injuries, but none that would need immediate medical attention; Jared had a bloody nose and a black eye, which was swelling to create a small mountain on his face. Antonia didn't seem to have many injuries besides some bloodied knuckles, while Brice had a large bruise forming on his head and dried blood coated his left arm. Lydia had a black eye and a puffy lip, but other than that seemed alright, if Emily didn't count the fact that she was out cold. It took much more time than it should have to make it through the hallway with Brice and Emily dragging Lydia along with them, but they moved as swiftly as possible, agreeing to exit through the door in which they had initially entered the facility. Keeping quiet, they neared it, hoping against hope that the other scientists really had been sent away to another facility, that they had conquered everyone there. The door was becoming closer by the minute, by the second, and the small windows allowed squares of light to shine in onto the floors. The squares were almost under their feet, so close, Emily staring at them as she struggled under the weight of her friend. But to her dismay, they suddenly disappeared, and Jared bumped into her as he backed up, stepping on her toes and pushing her back with his strong arm. Emily peered over his right shoulder, and standing in front of the doors were two guards holding real guns and aiming the weapons at the legs of each Plug. The guards still couldn't kill the Plugs...but they could hurt them.

# CHAPTER THIRTY-THREE

A single shot was fired before anyone had the chance to move, directly into Troy's leg, sending the rest of the group into a panic. Dropping to the floor, Antonia rolled up his jean pants and examined the bullet as blood dripped onto the floor around him. Emily and Brice laid Lydia down beside him. Using their bodies as a shield for the two on the ground, they aimed their guns and shot.

A scene of complete chaos broke out as Jared attempted to hit the guns out of the guards' hands. Managing to make contact with one, he sent it clattering to the floor and dove for it, Brice and Emily covering him as they fired. His sweaty hand grasped for the handle of the weapon and met it, Jared wrapping his fingers around the metal and turning onto his back to shoot. His aim wasn't the best, but now, it was three versus two. He sent bullets flying as Emily and Brice jumped out of the way with their weapons firing rapidly. Two shots hit the left foot of the female guard, another hitting the right arm of the male guard; as they stood stunned for a moment, Brice and Emily raced back towards Lydia. Antonia and Jared helped Troy to his feet and frantically forced their way through to the door. Wielding his gun, Brice waved it through the air and smashed the butt of the gun against the shoulders of one of the men, feeling it crack against bone and elbowing him so that he fell to the floor. They were finally crossing the threshold of the door, and as they did they could feel themselves stumble quicker and quicker in desperation. Troy groaned in agony as Antonia and Jared encouraged him to keep going. Having found an easier way to hold Lydia, Brice and Emily were able to move along the streets at the same pace as the others, racking their brains to remember where exactly their hiding spot was. Reaching a familiar looking store, they turned into the dark road behind it to find Mitch sitting nervously. He seemed shocked to see them, giving a short nod to Emily and pulling himself to his feet using the brick wall.

"Glad you made it," he coughed, flashing a smile and moving forward. "What happened to them?" Motioning to Lydia and Troy, he looked up towards Emily and raised his brows questioningly.

"Troy got shot, Lydia's out cold, and we need to get the hell out of here," she panted, her hair matted down against her damp forehead. Heavy breaths shook her entire body as she shifted Lydia on her shoulder, turning around with Brice and beginning to hurry down the street. "C'mon, they're probably sending people," she urged.

Mitch took a glance back at the facility and then at Lydia and Troy, running in front of Emily and putting his hands up. "Shouldn't we help them first, get them okay to actually move and stuff?" He seemed to be stalling for something, but Emily shook the thought from her head.

"No, we need to go, it's way more dangerous to stay. We can help them with their injuries later, first we need to get out of here." There was a pleading tone in her voice that sent a shiver down Mitch's back and his heart suffered a sharp pang, but he pressed on.

"Are you sure? I don't know about this, Emily."

"Definitely."

With a loud sigh, Mitch bent over to grab his pack and straightened up slowly, his shoulders slouched. As he took one last glance towards the facility in the distance, he stepped forward to join the group.

"Alright, where are we going?" Brice asked, looking around at the buildings surrounding them. "I guarantee you they're sending people out right now."

"Well, we can't keep running around in plain sight, that's where they'll be looking first," answered Antonia. The wheels in her brain spun rapidly as she tried to think of a place to stay, a place where they wouldn't be found.

"Wait…" Jared's eyes glazed over as if he were having a vision of some sort. "I have an idea."

Antonia had turned to face him quickly and met his eyes. "What is it?"

"There was a woman, on the train. She must've been heading to the city, too, and she gave me this!" Jared fumbled in his pocket and pulled out a crumpled sheet of paper, unfolding it. "151 Gold Street," he read aloud.

"Can we trust this woman?" Brice interjected suspiciously. "I mean, we don't really know how she heard about us in the first place. What if she's one of them? How else would she even be aware of the program? It's top secret."

"We don't have any other options," Emily sighed regretfully. "We need help, and we need it now. We can't keep doing this alone," she huffed.

"Then, let's go," Antonia urged.

Brice still sounded wary about the idea of relying on some mystery lady. "It's not that easy. We've got to find the building on Gold Street."

"I might be able to get us there," argued Antonia.

"How would you know the way?" Emily asked desperately.

"Trust me…I've done my prep. I…I found a few maps in my advisor's room last week, and I think I remember seeing Gold Street marked down. Just give me a second."

"We have to keep moving," Brice insisted. "Think while we go." He adjusted his grip on Lydia.

# CHAPTER THIRTY-FOUR

Lydia was beginning to come to, her eyes blinking many times before she got her feet underneath her. She took a short, gasping breath. Her arms flailed as she escaped from Emily and Brice's grip and turned quickly, staring at the street. Realizing that they had escaped the facility, she crouched down and began to breathe slowly, closing her eyes and standing back up. "What happened? Is everyone okay?" She sounded completely exhausted, the effects of the tranquilizer still wearing off.

"We got out…and, no, not everyone's okay, not exactly. Troy's hurt, we're trying to find the woman from the train, and we need to get the bullet out of Troy's leg." Emily peered down at the blood seeping through his jeans. Troy's eyes were drooping, and he lost his footing for a moment before standing back up.

"I…I think I'm gonna pass out," he said weakly, hunching over and vomiting loudly. His face turned a pale white, and he slouched back against the ground. Lydia pulled food and water out of her pack, pouring water onto Troy's forehead.

"Eat, drink, Troy, you're losing a lot of blood." Lydia's voice was shaky and breathless, and she handed crackers to him. "We need to hurry." She looked desperately up at Antonia, for once relying on someone other than herself to take control. Pulling off her jacket, Lydia threw the cloth over Troy's leg and pressed down on the wound.

Antonia turned herself around in a circle and then closed her eyes, letting her hands draw streets in the air in front of her. Suddenly, her eyes popped open, and she let out a deep breath.

"I know where to go," Antonia spoke up, a new energy taking over her mind.

"Lead the way," said Lydia.

The group rushed through the city, desperate to reach Jane's home, but afraid of what they might find.

The Rixtonne Apartment Buildings were incredibly rundown, but solid and sturdy. Almost every window was encrusted with dirt, and withering flowers formed an outline around the perimeter. The first set of doors were unlocked, and the wind blew them open and closed, one of them hanging on its hinges. A thicker pair of doors came after these, and they were locked tightly shut. No one seemed to be inside, and Antonia turned to Emily and Brice, who were struggling to keep Troy on his feet. Lydia, Jared, and Mitch were right behind them, waiting for instructions from Antonia, who stood up quickly and ran towards the wall.

"We've got to use these buzzers," she groaned, motioning to a huge panel of buttons. "They call up to the different apartments and…it's the only way we can get to Jane. Jared, do you remember the sound of her voice?" she asked desperately.

He nodded with determination and urged Antonia to begin.

With a sigh, she clicked the first buzzer. A harsh beeping noise burst from the panel. There was no answer from the first apartment, or the second, or the third. When a voice came on the fourth attempt, Antonia started. A woman's voice came through the panel's speaker.

"Hello?" it asked in an annoyed tone.

Antonia turned to Jared rapidly. "Is it her?!" she whispered.

Jared shook his head. "Hang up" he mouthed.

Antonia clicked the adjacent button.

Someone's yawn came through the speaker. "What do you want?"

Raising her eyebrows at Jared, Antonia held her breath.

"Nope," sighed Jared.

The next six attempts proved fruitless as well. The buzzing noise that came with each call gave Antonia a headache, and she ran her hand along her temple to soothe it. Crossing her fingers silently, she pressed the eleventh button. This time, the voice came quickly. "Who is it?" it whispered in a harsh and urgent tone, like it's owner had been waiting for this very call.

Jared nodded his head. "It's got to be her," he muttered, more to himself than anyone else. "We can't wait any longer, anyways." Motioning to Troy, he solemnly convinced Antonia and the rest of the Plugs to take the risk. "He needs help," he hissed.

Turning back to the buzzer, Antonia spoke into it. "Ja-Jane?" Her voice shook with anticipation.

Jared went to the buzzer and stood with his mouth close, obviously desperate now. "It's us. It's me, and we need your help. Let us up."

"I knew it," the voice boomed triumphantly. The call clicked off.

The Plugs could only hope that she'd let them in. Antonia tried the locked doors again, and the one on the right swung open. She sprinted to the long, winding staircase and began the dash to Jane's apartment. With her hand on the railing, Antonia began the long climb, closely followed by the group. Her headache raged on, but they were almost there, only a couple more flights of stairs, and they finally reached the sixth floor, opening the door to the musty hallway. It was quiet, the lights above flickering randomly. Leading the group down the hallway, Antonia finally stopped in front of a door that hovered slightly ajar. They were there; room six-hundred thirty-three. Antonia raised her hand in a fist and knocked loudly. Her knuckles had barely hit the door when it burst open.

A short grin flashed over Jane Simmal's face when she saw the Plugs in the doorway of her cluttered apartment. Peering behind Antonia to Troy, she stepped aside quickly and allowed the Plugs into the room. A crooked lampshade sat in the corner with nothing beneath it, three candles with cracked glass containers sitting on a small table in front of the biggest piece of furniture in the room: an overstuffed, red, shabby couch. Emily and Brice hurried to it, depositing Troy onto it and sprinting towards the woman. She was already hurrying back with a short knife, dull scissors, rubbing alcohol, and two long strands of cloth.

"What are you doing? He was shot, please, he needs help!" urged Emily, staring at the knife suspiciously. Emily had a weapon of her own, and she held it in front of her defensively, side stepping towards the pale Troy.

"Oh, don't be stupid, I'm getting the bullet out!" cried the old woman, rushing towards him and cutting away the fabric around where the bullet had lodged itself. The skin was a bloody mess beneath the jeans. The rest of the group watched carefully for any signs that this woman really wasn't on their side, stepping closer to her as she handed Troy a washcloth. "Scream into this," she instructed as Troy fumbled to bite down on the cloth.

"Hey, what'd you do that for?!" Lydia shouted loudly, taking a step towards Jane and raising her knife threateningly.

"Shhh," she held her finger to her lips, turning towards Troy and speaking over her shoulder. "It's going to hurt, and I'm not sure how loud his screams will be. We don't want him to be heard."

Nodding reluctantly, Lydia stepped away and folded her arms, watching as Jane located the bullet and left to find a towel. Brice could hear the water running as she soaked it in warm water, and he stepped closer to Lydia, leaning towards her and whispering in her ear. "Anything happens, we fight, okay? No different just because she's an old lady. I…I just don't want Troy getting hurt again."

Before Lydia could respond, Brice stepped back and crossed his arms, tilting his head forward to watch Troy's face. Jared, Antonia, Mitch and Emily stayed silent, and they stood behind the couch, facing Lydia and Brice.

Jared's face was a crimson red, and his hands squeezed the couch's back tightly, fingers turning white. He turned away from the cushions, running his hands through his hair impatiently as Jane shut the water off. "Would you please hurry up? If you couldn't tell, our friend kinda got shot!" His voice was thin, as if he were on the verge of tears, and he stayed facing away from the couch until the woman returned.

Clearing away the blood, Jane cleaned the spot around the bullet wound and looked up towards Troy, who was laying there with his eyes closed. Deciding it would be better to do the whole process quickly, she positioned the small knife on the outer edge of the metal and suddenly pressed underneath it, wedging out the bullet as it fell to the side. Blood began to rush out of the wound, and Troy was up, screaming through the cloth, his muffled shouts sending the group a step back.

A single tear streaked down Emily's dirt stained face, and she reached for Mitch's hand, but it was limp, and he didn't squeeze back. Her insides shuddered at the sight of her friend in so much pain, and her body shook. With a stony face, Mitch stared on, his other hand resting inside his pocket. Jared buried his head in the musty couch, his nails digging into the fabric, and Antonia was standing with her hands over her ears, biting her lip and looking sympathetically towards Troy every few moments. Kneeling besides the couch, Brice and Lydia held Troy's hand, squeezing it to remind him that they were still there. Jane continued to wrap the cloth around his leg, leaving to find another when the blood soaked through.

Heaving breaths and groans erupted from Troy's chest, pain enveloping everything around him until he felt like he was in a room full of blackness, a room that kept closing in upon him. Tears squeezed out of his tightly shut eyes, and Troy felt them trail down his cheeks and fall onto the thin pillow his head rested upon. The only hint he had that he was not alone was the occasional squeezing of his hand. Eventually, exhaustion overtook him in a crashing wave, drowning him in visions of guns and scents of blood. His arms, legs, and mind felt tired beyond what he thought possible, and Troy allowed himself to welcome it openly, falling into a well-deserved sleep.

# CHAPTER THIRTY-FIVE

The Plugs and Mitch gathered in Jane's small room, telling her that they needed a second to talk. Emily shut the door quietly and flung herself towards Antonia, wrapping her arms around her in a hug. Lydia joined in along with Jared and Brice, creating a group hug that lasted for a few minutes, during which Antonia began to cry. Relief that they were free, all of them together, for at least a little while, joy that they had succeeded in saving their friend, and pure exhaustion.

Once the hug ceased, Antonia went to sit on the single bed, pushing her hair behind her ears and taking a breath. "Thank you, guys. Thank you so much. I thought maybe...I thought I'd never get out." Her voice shook with emotion, and she had to finish her sentence quickly to keep herself from crying again. Wiping away any remaining tears, she looked up at the group of them and glanced at Mitch. "Sorry, but...who are you?" Her eyes turned stony and curious.

Mitch looked towards Emily with panicked eyes, and she nodded encouragingly, smiling at him with ease.

"Uh, I helped Emily get out. Of her facility, I mean."

Antonia nodded, satisfied with his explanation, and then turned towards the rest of the group, resting her chin in her palm. "So, what happened while I was gone?" She said it as if they hadn't just escaped a dangerous situation, as if she had simply been out buying coffee and just come back for breakfast. Her eyebrows were raised, and she smiled expectantly, waiting for someone to speak.

"Well…uh, we've kind of got some issues, and we've gotta tell you quickly." Lydia stepped forward and ran her hand through her hair slowly, rubbing her tired eyes and blinking a few times to clear out the fogginess.

"Great." Standing up, Antonia turned to smooth out the spot where she'd been sitting and turned back towards Lydia.

"Okay, so we're currently being broadcast all over the news," Lydia started.

Antonia frowned slightly, crossing her arms and looking down towards the floor, obviously thinking.

"Plus, we kind of were attacked before we got you, and Mitch's life was threatened, but that's it. So other than that, it's been smooth sailing."

# CHAPTER THIRTY-SIX

"And…what's the plan?" Kicking her shoes off into the corner of the room, Antonia sat in the middle of the floor and waited for the rest to do the same.

"As of now, we don't really have one," Jared admitted. "We can't go back to the facilities, and we can't just pretend we're normal people."

"Can we leave the country? Change our names, our appearances?" Antonia's eyes lit up with hope.

"They're never gonna stop looking for us," Emily lamented. "And I can't just pretend this never happened. I have to do something to stop the P.E.I."

"Then what do we do to end this?" Brice huffed.

"Well…there's no real way to end it unless we destroy the root of the project. Running away won't ruin everything for them…they still have their research at the headquarters," Emily said. "Lydia, what do you think?"

They all faced Lydia, listening expectantly for her idea.

"I don't know…I was thinking we could destroy the facilities, and then…" Lydia shook her head decisively, changing her mind about something. Picking anxiously at her cuticles, she sat on her hands and sighed, staring down at the stained carpet floor. "What do you guys think?"

Emily bit her lip. "I mean…don't get me wrong, I like the idea. But are we really ready to go after the headquarters? We barely got out of the Albany facility."

"We'd need help…some bigger force," Lydia agreed.

Antonia nodded slowly, the wheels turning in her mind. "You're right…we need soldiers of some sort. Maybe Jane's got some allies, a group or something." Shrugging, she continued. "She can't be the only one who disagrees with the P.E.I., I guess."

Jared sighed loudly, overwhelmed by the entire prospect. "She did say that she knows other people who hate the P.E.I., who'd be willing to fight. I'm not sure what that really means, though, or if they'll be on board."

Emily was the next to pitch in. "They can help us with our plan. I'm sure of it."

Raising her eyebrows, Lydia put her chin in her hands. "How?"

"Well, by becoming a sort of army, of course. They'll help us destroy the headquarters."

Brice rolled his eyes as he spoke. "It's not going to be that easy. How do we know if they can fight? How do we know that they won't turn us in?"

"We can't do this alone," Jared argued. "We have to take this risk."

"It's too high a risk," muttered Brice.

"Can't you just have a little hope, please?" Emily shot Brice a look.

"Whatever."

"Let's go talk to Jane. We need to learn if we can get all these group members to meet up here, and soon." Lydia walked to the door and turned the knob, pulling it open and following everyone out. "There's only so much time until we're found." The door slammed shut.

Later, the loudest sound in the apartment was silverware scraping against plates as Jane, Mitch, and the Plugs sat down to a thrown together dinner. It was silent as everyone ate anxiously in the dim room. Mitch was confused about what exactly was going on, and the Plugs were waiting for the right time to reveal their plan. Jane Simmal seemed not to mind the silence, slurping loudly from her chipped coffee mug and staring out the windows across the room. Her white hair was crimped, most of it pulled away from her face in a bun. Still, a few strands managed to escape and dangle by her cheeks. She held a worn out but satisfied expression on her face as she watched the sun set, and when it finally disappeared behind the closest skyline, she stood up and pushed her chair in.

"Wait!" Emily held her hand up, eyes pleading with Jane to sit down again. "We need to talk."

A smile washed across Jane's face, her eyelids creasing at the corners. "Ah, yes, I thought you would want to." Taking another sip of her drink, she gently laid the cup on the table and folded her arms.

The group stared at her with desperation; Lydia took this as her cue to speak.

"Well, we agree with you. We've decided that the only way to stop the experiment is to destroy the headquarters, which means destroying all their data and research. That way, we can at least slow down the P.E.I. from creating more Plugs. But, we need help. You mentioned that you have a group, one that feels the same way we do. We need them to help us bring down the P.E.I." Lydia paused and nervously coughed. She waited for Jane's response.

Jane nodded, stood up, and exited the room. "Just a minute," she called over her shoulder as she left. Returning with a notebook in hand, she set it on the table and flipped it open. A page full of names and phone numbers came into view, and she trailed her finger along the side, stopping when it hit the last name "Guadalupe."

"We'll start with her," Jane muttered.

"Wait, wait…you need to tell us what you're doing. First you miraculously take a bullet out of Troy's legs, and now you're basically talking in code. Who are you, and what do you get out of destroying the headquarters? And…and who the hell are those people?" Lydia gestured impatiently at the notebook.

Slowly, Jane let her hand flatten against the page and closed her eyes, reigning in her anger. "Trust me, I wouldn't be helping you if there weren't something in it for me. I'm not some noble saint who wants to save the world." She let out a heavy sigh. "My son…he was one of the scientists in the beginning, when the P.E.I. was just being formed. He thought he was helping—he was a good boy. But, when he saw what they were doing, when he saw how they were treating children, he tried to get out. I remember him calling me and saying that he couldn't stand it anymore. I told him that it was too dangerous, that he needed to wait it out. He didn't, and they killed him. He knew too much." Jane shook her head angrily and slammed her fist on the table with rage. "And now, I won't sleep until I have one of those animals' heads on a spear."

# CHAPTER THIRTY-SEVEN

The table shook when Jane hit it, and her mug fell to the floor, coffee splattering. Emily was the first to respond.

"I'm…I'm sorry, Jane. But, we can't kill anyone. We'll get them back for what they've done to us, to you, to countless people. But first you need to tell us who you're planning on asking for help."

Taking a deep breath, Jane calmed herself and straightened out the notebook. I have some friends who I met long ago. They've all suffered under the Initiative's hands, and I'm sure they'll jump at the opportunity to avenge their loved ones."

Lydia nodded, encouraged by the idea. "Sounds good. Let's get this thing going, then."

Jane nodded in agreement and stood to retrieve her phone. "Okay, first I'm calling Maria Guadalupe. She's an expert shooter…really knows her way around firearms. Her husband left her for his work at the facilities."

Brice grimaced in shock. How many of these terrible stories were they going to hear tonight?

The buttons on the phone chimed as Jane typed in Maria's number. As the phone dialed, the entire room hung on edge. Finally, a woman's voice answered.

"Jane? Been a while, what are you up to?"

"Well…a lot, Maria. I think you're gonna want to hear this. I've got them here."

"You don't mean…?"

"Yes, the Plugs. They're on our side now. Get the team back together. This experiment's about to burn to the ground, and we're gonna set the match. Everyone needs to be at my place by tomorrow night. We've gotta act fast."

"Jane, you can't be serious. How would they be in your apartment? You must be crazy," Maria scoffed. Still, the fact that she stayed on the line gave the Plugs some hope.

Brice shot up in his seat and reached for the phone, grabbing it out of Jane's hand and pressing his mouth to the receiver. "We're…we're here. And we're ready to fight back."

# CHAPTER THIRTY-EIGHT

The phone calls finally came to an end hours later. They managed to convince nineteen people to attend an urgent meeting at Jane's apartment, whose hearts, full of vengeance, made for deadly weapons.

Jane handed out all her spare blankets to the Plugs, but the temperature of the room dropped as the night went on. Apparently, Jane hadn't paid her heating bills. The conditions were the worst for Troy, who managed to progress to a steady sitting position on the couch. The rest of the group gathered around him, reluctant to let their backs touch the cold wooden floor, but they gave in, lying down gradually and staring up at the ceiling. Mitch was sleeping nearby, and Emily stood up quietly, moving to sit beside him.

"What's up?" she whispered into his ear, her breath hot against his neck.

His eyes drifted to meet hers, and he smiled. "Honestly, I'm pretty scared." Mitch's voice sounded afraid even as he whispered, and his eyes began to glimmer in the night.

"I am too." She took his hand and squeezed it. "But, Mitch, I need to ask…what's wrong?" The question hovered in the air and she hurried to fill the silence. "You just seem different, y'know, from when we first met. I've just noticed that you're quieter, and more…hesitant."

Mitch's eyes opened widely as she spoke, but they had returned to their normal size by the end of her sentence. "I'm just scared, Em. I promise." A single tear escaped his eye and began trailing its way down his cheek, a wet streak left in its path.

Emily moved her thumb to wipe it away, kissing Mitch's forehead and lying down a few feet from him. "I'm here, Mitch. Don't be afraid."

"Don't you ever doubt yourself?"

"Every second. I still don't know if I'm doing the right thing here. I still feel horrible, because every day I'm gone, I know that I'm ruining the lives of those scientists. Some of them were nice to me. Some of them just wanted to change the world, like us. And I wasted their time and their money and their futures. I don't know if a handful of people's freedom is worth that. I don't know. Maybe I've ruined everything. Maybe ten years from now people will be talking about the selfish teenager who doomed the country. It's so stupid to think like that, but I can't help it. I can't help but remember how they used to call me the solution. And I'm ripping that away from them. From you."

"You're not ripping anything away from me, Em. I'll make my choice, just like you'll make yours." He let out the sentence in the midst of a sigh.

Across the room, Lydia's breathing didn't slow, and her eyes stared steadily up at the ceiling. Hesitant to allow herself to let down her guard, Lydia kept her eyes wide open. Although she knew that she needed rest, she couldn't allow herself to put anyone in danger by falling asleep. It seemed like the rest of the Plugs saw her as the leader, and she felt that pressure heavily weigh upon her at this crucial time. It was like a constant squeezing on her insides, tensing up every muscle until she felt like a rubber band about to snap.

It seemed like hours until Lydia was able to fall asleep, hearing the breathing of others slow to a lull over time. When she finally closed her eyes, she made sure everyone else was asleep. Maybe they wouldn't see her let her guard down after all.

# CHAPTER THIRTY-NINE

When the day began, Antonia was sitting at the table, silently watching the glass of water in her hands.

Jared shifted in his sleep, finally awakening and nearing the table where she sat. The others were still asleep, and he spoke in whispers. "Morning, Annie."

Antonia let out a short laugh. "I told you not to call me that," she protested. Jared had always teased her with that name back in their early years at the facilities. A scientist had called her Annie once by mistake, and for some reason, the Plugs found it hilarious; no one ever really got their names wrong at the facilities.

"Yeah, but that was five years ago. I thought maybe you'd changed your mind," Jared joked back, elbowing her lightly.

"Whatever." Shaking her head a little, Antonia looked down at her wrist and circled it. She winced in pain.

"What's wrong?!" Jared noticed her grimace and took her wrist lightly. Small red scratches circled it, and he took in a quick breath. "What did they do to you?"

Antonia pulled away, her face red now. "Nothing, it's…it's not a big deal, Jared."

"The scratches are recent. Is it…is it because of us, Annie? Did they try to get information out of you?"

Glancing at him apologetically, Antonia looked away in shame. "It's not your fault. They just did this, um, this tactic, like an experiment."

"A tactic? Like, torture?"

"No, no…I mean, I guess, kind of. It was just some serum and they had my wrist and legs locked up, that's all." Even as she spoke, tears filled her eyes.

"Oh, God, Antonia I'm so sorry." Jared's voice rose as he shook his head in shock.

"Jared, be quiet! You've got to promise you won't tell anyone else—I don't want them to feel bad."

"You should really tell them, maybe Jane has medicine for your cuts or something."

"I don't care. Don't you see?"

"What do you mean?"

"It's just that I…" She stopped, gathering her thoughts. "I'm upset because I understand why they did it. I don't know why I can forgive them so easily." Dropping her hands, Antonia moved closer to Jared and hugged him tightly. "So, do you promise?"

"Huh?" Jared asked, hugging her back.

"That you won't tell the others."

"Fine."

***

The day passed painstakingly slow. A nervous energy filled the apartment; all of the residents tried desperately to hide their stress, but it was impossible with Jane's friends arriving that very evening. The only question on the Plugs' minds was how success was even possible. How would they manage to wipe out the headquarters and the information contained there? How would they work up the courage to attempt it in the first place?

***

"Maria Guadalupe, pleased to make your acquaintance." A woman with a thick accent and curly black hair had just been welcomed into Jane's apartment. She reached forward and shook each of the Plugs' hands, gripping them for a moment longer than necessary. With a curt nod, she retreated to the table and started to unload weapons onto the ground beside her seat.

Emily shifted her weight from foot to foot nervously, fidgeting with her hair as another knock came at the door. Moving to answer it, Jane pulled it open timidly and then embraced a tall man with a wild goatee. His voice was raspy as he murmured his greetings to Jane and pulled away.

"Hey. I'm Jordan." He acknowledged the Plugs and strode over to a seat by the table without another word.

The rest of Jane's guests arrived in the same way: serious, quiet, and ready to fight. By eight o'clock, the makeshift team was gathered around the table and ready to plan.

Jane sat up straighter in her seat and cleared her throat. "I think we all know why we're here. The time has finally come to get our revenge and do what we've believed is right all along…to take out the P.E.I. The Plugs have told me the headquarters are in Brooklyn. We need a strong plan. So now is the time to brainstorm, to throw all your expertise and knowledge out on the table."

Silence filled the room for a moment. But soon enough, a buff woman with an assertive voice spoke up. A fiery vibe radiated from her; not only was she ready to fight, but she was eager, even excited. The Plugs couldn't help but wonder what had hardened her heart so much.

"I'm Angeline…and I'm an expert at crafting bombs." That earned her a murmur of approval from the crowd, and a small tremor from Antonia.

And so, the group went around the table, one by one announcing the role they could play in the final attack on the facilities. Some spoke about their hatred for the immoral nature of the Initiative, while others even apologized to the Plugs for their suffering.

"I'm Gabe. I am a computer expert…there's no system I can't hack," he announced confidently. But if Emily looked into his eyes, she could tell that he was afraid. And that scared her.

The list went on, and by the end, Lydia couldn't sit still.

"So…what are we actually going to do?" It was clear that Lydia was growing impatient.

"We fight our way through, of course." Jordan shrugged like this was the obvious answer.

Angeline raised her hand. "Why can't we just bomb the whole place?"

"I think that the Plugs should all pretend to give themselves up, distract the scientists from the headquarters," Maria suggested with confidence. "I know Vicky here could hack the entire database with access to one of their computers. I could destroy most of their equipment and files with fire. Once we get inside, all hell breaks loose."

"Wait, slow down!" Emily cried. "We're not killing anyone…understood?" She stood up abruptly to emphasize her point.

A wave of disappointment passed through the crowd, and Emily sighed loudly. "I like that idea. But we need to be one hundred percent sure that we evacuate the building before we destroy it. That means that one of us needs to pull the fire alarm before we start burning the place down. Plus, we need to assign groups and make sure we all know exactly what we're doing. We've only got one shot at this, so we simply can't screw it up."

Jordan scoffed. "No pressure."

Gabe rolled his eyes. "Why can't we kill people? We put ourselves in danger if we get too close."

"If we kill them, that makes us even worse than the scientists!" Crossing her arms, Antonia clenched her jaw. "We're fighting clean. That's that."

Murmurs passed through the crowd.

Lydia clapped her hands, making everyone jump. "Alright, then. Let's get started. Maria, Josh, Fiona, you said you're experts with firearms. So did Freddy, Ray, and Simaree. We're gonna need you for defense. Once everyone's evacuated, hold the fort down. You can be our backup, but only if we really need to shoot. And you need to supply us all with guns, but only as self-defense, only if it really comes down to it. No unnecessary deaths, got it?"

The six adults nodded and began talking among themselves, planning which firearms they could supply and train with.

Antonia pointed at the people beside them. "You three said you're explosives experts. We need you to plan how to wreck the headquarters, but not any surrounding buildings. And you four...you said your specialty was hand to hand combat. You should be our first line of defense, in case anything happens while Vicky and Gabe are destroying the database. That's what we need to do first. I'm sure that all the scientists' information is stored in computers in the headquarters. Second, we need to destroy any physical files, equipment, medical samples. Destroy the information, destroy the project."

# CHAPTER FORTY

"This is the plan." Lydia jabbed her finger at a large piece of paper. "You need to get us to the headquarters, but stay behind and watch. Once we get inside the building," she motioned to herself and the rest of the Plugs, ""we create a diversion. Everyone freaks out, we distract the scientists and the guards…that's when you all break in." Lydia looked up at the combat fighters and hackers; they were all hunched over the page with focused expressions. "While we work on wiping the database, the combat fighters work on destroying the building."

"Okay," Maria responded. "But how?"

"Angeline, how much damage can your bombs do?"

"As much as you need them to." Angeline crossed her arms. "I like a good challenge."

"Fantastic." Lydia turned to the hackers. "Vicky, the Plugs and I will meet up with you and Gabe. Just focus on hacking into the system and destroying all the files, and we'll come to you. The rest of you stay outside, make sure everything runs smoothly, and keep people out of the building. Got it?"

"We need specifics, Lydia. How're you gonna get in? How're you gonna get away from the guards?" Jordan leaned forward, eyebrows furrowed.

"Getting in will be easy," she promised. "I have a foolproof idea."

"And that would be?"

Lydia smiled. "We'll be the bait."

"So, you're gonna hand yourselves over?" Maria sounded unsure. "How will you get away from the guards?"

Lydia turned to Jordan. "Would you be down to play dress-up?"

"I'm down for anything that'll take the place out."

# CHAPTER FORTY-ONE

"What's this?" Antonia hovered over Angeline. Red and blue wires twisted and looped as Angeline's fingers flew quickly.

Angeline didn't talk much. Her eyes were always narrowed, focused, and she could never sit still.

"It's the bomb. The one to blow up the headquarters."

"No, I mean this." Antonia pointed at a little picture in a golden locket.

"It's Mirem. My godson. Well, really my son. I couldn't have children." Angeline stopped moving for a moment. "I adopted him when his parents died."

Antonia had never seen her slow down for so long. "That's...nice."

"Mm." Angeline wasn't really listening anymore.

"Why's he in the locket? If you don't mind me asking, I mean." Usually when someone's face lived in a locket, it meant they lived nowhere else.

"He's dead, if that's what you're getting at, hon."

"I'm so sorry." Antonia meant it.

"I would be, too."

"Wh-what?"

"If I felt I was a part of his death. Which, I'm not saying it's your fault, but...I know it's how you feel."

"How would you know that?"

"Because it's how I feel." A sigh. "At first, I encouraged this new project. I told him it was the opportunity of a lifetime, a chance to make a difference. I thought I'd done it, really done it: raised a good man, a smart man who would change the world." Angeline swiped at her eye and kept turning the wires. "He wouldn't be dead if I hadn't convinced him to go. He said it was my choice; my opinion would make up his mind. But then, there was this one experiment on you guys that he did that pushed him over the edge. He wouldn't tell me what it was exactly in his letter."

"I thought that people couldn't write letters to outsiders."

"They can't. And I wasn't supposed to know that it was a suicide. The P.E.I. told me he had an aneurysm. They shipped me all his old clothes, all his shoes and picture frames and bow ties. But nothing important. I knew he wouldn't go so quietly. He'd want to reach me somehow, even if it was the last thing he did on that hospital bed. So, I searched and searched and searched through his stuff. It took me three months, but eventually I found something. He'd folded a piece of paper underneath the sole of his dress shoes. It was a suicide letter. He apologized so many times. He said sorry, over and over and over."

"It wasn't your fault. You thought you were helping him, back then."

"I did, I swear I did. It wasn't until he died that I realized how cruel the project really was. How do you even sleep at night, with all those awful memories in your head?"

Antonia forced herself to laugh, but the noise came out dark, sharp. "I don't sleep that much. But when I do, I usually dream or imagine things. I like to think of the sky. I pretend I'm a bird, and I'm seeing the world. It's not so bad when I think of that."

"I don't sleep either."

Antonia saw the dark circles under Angeline's eyes. "You should try dreaming, too. It helps."

Later on, Antonia heard another story from Maria.

Maria recounted her experience with the P.E.I. in a quiet, harsh tone, never meeting eyes with Antonia. For Maria, it was a loved one named Louis, not Mirem, that had broken her.

Maria and Louis met in high school. Louis played on the baseball team, and Maria played soccer. She used to go to his games after her own. She used to make him posters and sit on the bleachers to cheer him on. They used to go to the pizza parlor and buy big pepperoni slices and share them with fizzing soda. Then, they'd see a movie and kiss in the back row. That was Maria's life for a long while.

When he was eighteen, Louis told Maria that he loved her. He kissed her nose and forehead and hugged her long and hard. He said they'd never be apart and he'd never leave her, because one day they'd get married under a big willow tree. Willow trees were their favorite, because there were so many in their small town and the waving branches were the best to have picnics under.

Then they went to college. Maria and Louis went together. Their parents said it was stupid of them to be so attached, but Maria knew it was true love.

When they were twenty-two, they decided to get married. Maria had hope; she knew it was meant to be. They married under a willow tree, and their life began together. Louis and Maria bought a quaint yellow house with a big backyard.

Louis turned twenty-eight. He worked at the hospital down the street from their house. The town knew him for his talent. Maria was so, so proud.

One day, he came home to the little yellow house with a white letter in his hand. It was thick paper with a seal. It looked very official. Louis told Maria that the government had asked him to join their new project, the PLUGS Energy Initiative. They'd have to move, but it was all worth it, he promised. He would be part of something big, something huge, something so much more important than anything he'd ever been a part of.

That hurt Maria. She asked if she was important, if their friends and house were important. She said she didn't think they should move, that she didn't want to leave their lives behind.

They argued for two weeks. Louis couldn't believe that Maria wouldn't make this sacrifice for him. Maria couldn't believe Louis would value his job over his family.

On a quiet Thursday night, Louis got home six hours late. Maria sat in a big armchair, watching the clock. When Louis burst through the door, he held a piece of paper in his hand. Maria asked him where he'd been, why he hadn't told her about his night plans. He said he'd forgotten to let her know about a work dinner.

Louis' eyes were wild that night. He wouldn't go to sleep.

When Maria woke up, he was gone.

# CHAPTER FORTY-TWO

"Hand thrusts up, then jab the eyes." Jordan made the motion in the air, hooking up and then twisting his hand.

Lydia was awestruck. She'd always wanted to learn self-defense. The Plugs around her seemed less fascinated. When Jordan had suggested they learn some moves, they understood the necessity, but only Lydia and Brice thought it would be fun. Troy was getting better, but his leg still hurt too much to practice just yet. He sat in a nearby chair, observing.

Lydia copied Jordan's movement in the air. She imagined she was in the midst of a real fight.

Jordan walked down the row, adjusting their positions, letting them try the eye gouge move on him. He dodged the swings perfectly and coached them on each movement.

The next move was called the throat punch, according to Jordan. Lydia thought it was a stupid name, but she loved the trick itself: fake a right swing, then go for the Adam's apple.

Jordan walked down the row, adjusting their positions, letting them practice. Their progress was impressive, and Jordan was hopeful that they would be able to defend themselves well if it came to it.

Back in the kitchen, Angeline had finished making two bombs. They sat on the table, three feet away from Vicky and Gabe, who were heatedly discussing their tactics for breaking down firewalls. Across the room, Maria and Jane compared weapons, loading up all of the guns with bullets and organizing them by size. They would start distributing them soon.

The room had adopted an eager buzz; a sense of anticipation permeated the air, and everyone was immersed in their preparations. The army was excited for the opportunity to finally get revenge, but fully aware that this was its only shot to take out the P.E.I. for good. With that pressure came an unbreakable focus, a need for precision. If anything went wrong, their efforts would be ruined and the project would survive. But soon, the time for planning would come to a halt, and the time for execution would arrive.

# CHAPTER FORTY-THREE

Lydia sat alone in the bathroom, her back pressed against the wall as she splashed cool water against her flushed face. She didn't like to show it, but she was afraid. And the worst part of all was that she was afraid for everyone else, not herself. How could she lead these people into a fight that they had such little chance of winning? Her heart ached at the thought of how many of them could potentially be hurt. She felt guilty for thinking that way. She needed to think positively, act confident like she always did.

Suddenly, a short knock sounded against the door. Drying her face, Lydia took a deep breath and opened it calmly, hoping all traces of her tears had disappeared.

Brice stood at the door, still a little groggy from sleep and rubbing his eyes.

"What's up?" Lydia asked, hoping to seem relaxed.

"I heard you get up, and you've been gone a long time. I wanted to make sure you were okay," Brice shrugged, obviously a little embarrassed.

Instinctually opening her mouth to assure him that she was perfectly fine, Lydia stopped herself. This was Brice; one of her best friends in the entire world and one of the only people she could truly trust. And now, all she wanted was to be heard and to let out her feelings.

"I'm so scared, Brice. I'm so scared. Don't you feel terrible? We both know we can't win this fight, so why are we leading innocent people into it?!"

Brice pulled Lydia into a hug, and she rested her head against his shoulder, tears silently pouring down her face. It felt good, freeing.

"Everyone is," Brice whispered. "But we have a chance, and we've trained so hard. Maria and Jordan are prepared, Vicky and Gabe have thought up all of the possible scenarios...we're ready for this. It's for the best, Lydia. Imagine if they did to generation after generation what they did to us. The fight is what we need to end this inhumanity, even if in and of itself the fight is inhumane."

Nodding, Lydia accepted that there was no more running. It was time to fight back against the oppressors who had taken their lives. "No more lives stolen, no more freedom lost," she whispered earnestly.

# CHAPTER FORTY-FOUR

Their attack on headquarters was nearing and becoming a daunting reality. The days leading up to the planned attack went quickly, and by Thursday night, with the fighters all sleeping in Jane's apartment, the room was highly charged.

Although everyone was extremely nervous, Mitch looked utterly sick. His face had a green tint to it, and sweat was beading on his forehead and dripping down his nose. He had retreated from everyone and escaped to Jane's room, where he sat with his legs pulled to his chest and his arms wrapped around them.

Emily was the first to notice his absence, and she entered Jane's room unsteadily. Mitch seemed awfully out of sorts lately, and while she was curious, she was terrified to hear what was wrong.

He looked up quickly when she came into view. Standing up, he wiped his clammy hands on his pants and stared into Emily's eyes. His bottom lip was quivering slightly as if he were on the brink of tears, and she ran to envelop him in a hug. He didn't hug back, leaving his arms hanging limp by his sides.

"Mitch, honestly, just tell me. What is wrong with you?" Emily had pulled back to look into his eyes. They were filled with sorrow, and a hint of regret.

"Nothing, Emily! God, how many times do I need to tell you?! Will you please just leave me alone?!" His face was now turning a bright pink and his stance became tighter. "Just let me be. You barely even know me." He was obviously in distress, and he turned to the window, his hands shaking.

Taking a step back, Emily stumbled over her feet. "I'm sorry, Mitch...I didn't know that was how you felt." His words were like a knife, slashing her with every syllable.

Turning to face her, Mitch covered his face. "No, I'm sorry, Em, I'm so sorry. I didn't mean it."

"You don't need to be sorry for anything." A short silence was shared between them while she waited for a response. How could he change so suddenly?

The confusion in her eyes sent Mitch's heart plunging as he thought about the coming day. Ever since they'd met, life had been a complete whirlwind, and at this point, he wasn't sure who he was himself. But he hugged her, squeezing tightly before letting go and turning away to face the wall again. Conjuring up as calm a voice as he could, he took a deep breath. "You...you should go. I need to think."

It wasn't until he heard the door click shut that he slumped to the floor and began panicking once again.

# CHAPTER FORTY-FIVE

Friday morning came much too quickly for Brice. The risk was beginning to fully hit the team. Brice had always tried to be the one to motivate his friends, but he wasn't so sure he'd be able to do that today. Death doesn't become a real fear until it is right around the corner.

Jane's apartment was eerily quiet. The volunteer fighters had accepted that there was a chance they'd die in a couple of hours, and the weight of that realization settled on each and every person's shoulders. Jane herself sat quietly at the table, sipping coffee and looking around the room at the nervous face of each person. She was the calmest of everyone, a silent figure sitting alone.

Brice walked over to her slowly, interrupting her calm gaze. He had never been very fond of Jane; she was too ominous for his liking. But, now he needed her advice, and even he could admit to himself that she was very wise.

"Are we...doing the right thing?" The nervousness in his voice could be heard, and a frown stretched across his mouth. "I mean, for all these people. For them," he gestured to the people all around the room, making sure to keep his voice low.

"No, probably not. I'm sure a lot of them will get hurt." Jane placed her coffee down after taking one more sip.

"Wait, what?! Why did you suggest this, then?!' Brice's voice rose quickly as he glared back at her in anger.

"I didn't say you were doing the wrong thing for the general public. I said you were doing the wrong thing for them. For the country, you're doing the right thing. It's nineteen people versus the millions who make up this country. It's your choice who you want to protect."

"I'll protect everyone," Brice demanded indignantly.

"Then you've made your choice," Jane grinned proudly. "But it won't be easy, I can promise you that."

Suddenly, Brice found himself appreciating Jane a little more.

# CHAPTER FORTY-SIX

Right before the time came for them to journey to the headquarters, Lydia and Brice gathered all of the Plugs into a room.

Seeming much more distraught than usual, Lydia stood and spoke. "Since we may never see each other again if the P.E.I. captures us, I think that we should say our last words while we still can. Um...I'll go first." Waiting until everyone, including herself, had gathered into a circle on the floor, she finally began. "I know that we only met up recently, and I know that the circumstances have been pretty awful. But you guys are the ones who helped me through it all. I can be bossy, and I can be harsh, but I swear, it was only ever to protect you guys. Emily, Antonia...you're my sisters. And even though we might not have done traditional sister stuff, I can't imagine having it any other way. Brice, Jared, and Troy, you guys are my brothers." A tear had begun to travel down her cheek as she spoke, and for once, she didn't wipe it away. "That's...that's all I have to say." Her face was long, and she suddenly seemed like a little kid again, so afraid and overwhelmed by the future.

They all looked to Jared, who was sitting on Lydia's left, as he began to speak. "Without you guys, I have no idea how I would've made it through everything we've dealt with. I don't think I could have. You five, you've kept me from hitting rock bottom when I thought there were no other options." He coughed a few times to clear his throat. "So, I guess what I'm saying is, without you guys, I have no idea what my life would be or who I'd be." His hands shook a little and he clasped them together to steady them, staring towards the floor sadly.

Emily's voice sounded small as she reminisced about old times, when they all stayed at the same facility. She talked through her sniffles, saying, "We did everything we could, for ourselves and for each other, and I don't regret anything. We were handed nothing, and we made something." She twirled a loose string on the rug around her finger, ripping away the thread and watching it unravel.

Troy slung his arm around her shoulder. "I'm sorry we couldn't escape and live happily ever after...I know it's what we all wanted. But I'm not even sure if happily ever after exists anymore," he mumbled, defeated. "But what I do know is that you guys are my happiness, and I think I got pretty damn close to my happily ever after with you."

Lydia groaned affectionately. "You're such a sap."

An emptiness descended upon them. There was nothing left to say, nothing left to distract them from the inevitable.

The Plugs' voices were numb, as if they still weren't prepared for what was about to happen. No one truly could be prepared for this, this horrible fear of being separated again. It was a quiet but loud circle, the words spoken softly but the meaning so, so deafening.

They continued through the circle, the Plugs struggling to hold themselves together. By the end of it, everyone was in tears, huddled together in a tight hug. Their faces searched through one another's, desperately trying to capture this moment and hold onto it.

Preparing themselves for the final fight, they squeezed each other's shoulders one last time and listened to Emily whisper, "I love you guys." One by one they left Jane's room and motioned to the gathered people that it was time to leave, descending the many stairs of the building.

It was time for the end. And it was time to start a new beginning.

# CHAPTER FORTY-SEVEN

The train ride to the headquarters was uncomfortable, to say the very least. Mitch sat next to Emily, who kept glancing over at him nervously like he was some sort of basket case. He couldn't bring himself to look back at her, staring out of the window for the full ride. Building after building whizzed past. No one in the city had any idea what was about to happen. They had no idea that an experiment had been carried out right under their noses for seventeen years.

Suddenly, Emily began to speak softly to him, so gentle in her tone. "I know you're scared. I am too. But I just have this feeling deep inside that we can do it, if we work together. I just know it. I think everything has lead up to this, as crazy as that sounds."

"Do you really feel that way? Do you really think we have a shot at winning?" Mitch's eyes locked with hers.

"Of course I do. I'm positive that we can. As long as we know what side we're fighting for, there's nothing that can hold us back."

# CHAPTER FORTY-EIGHT

The air was crisp, and Emily breathed it in thankfully, hoping it would soothe her quickly mounting nerves. The building was only a hundred yards away, now, and she wanted to cherish what could be her last moments of freedom.

Although the Plugs were afraid, they felt numb and detached from their bodies, as if they were spectators of the scene being played out before them. All that they'd done had led up to this moment, and now they just needed to finish the job. But in the few moments before they neared the headquarters security, in the few steps before giving themselves up, it was hard not to feel doubt. What if their plan didn't work, and they were separated again? Would they need to live the rest of their days apart, with only a few good memories to keep them going? There wasn't enough time to think, and as the Plugs came closer to the facility, seven guards rushed up to them. Unlike before, the guards seemed to have full permission to use force with the Plugs.

And so, it was a moment later that Lydia was pushed face down onto the ground with a boot on her back. Spitting out dirt, she coughed and took a deep breath. For this plan to work, she needed to hold back her anger. She let her body relax and felt herself being pulled to her feet by another guard, the cold rim of a gun pressed against her back.

"Shut up and come with us" a guard shouted so loudly that Antonia cowered away. When he noticed her do this, he tightened his grip on her arms.

The Plugs were shoved towards the headquarters, a set of steely doors coming closer and closer. An overwhelming sense of dejavú washed over them.

And suddenly they were inside, hallway after hallway leading them to all too familiar places. The seven men pushed them further and further through the headquarters, and after the third turn, Brice realized that they were heading towards the operating rooms. They had to act now.

Brice and Jared swung around and wrenched their arms out of their captors' grips, throwing hard punches. Brice could feel his guard's nose crunch with the contact, and just like that two more guards were upon him, pushing him to the ground and holding down his arms and legs. Jared was wrestled to the floor as well, cheek pressed against the cool tiles. During all of the commotion, Emily slipped away. Nearing the wall, she pulled the fire alarm desperately and a shrill noise rang through the air. Brice and Jared continued to struggle, distracting the scientists just in time for Emily to return and slow her breathing. Body aching all over, Brice pushed himself to his feet and shook himself off. Jared let the guards wrench him off the floor. They were all red in the face now, and they turned right back around, cursing under their breath. Emily sighed in relief; they hadn't noticed her absence. As the guards herded the Plugs back through the door, Brice gave a small nod to her. They'd made it through the first step.

Back out the headquarters they went, scientists filing out behind them in a panicked manner. Their chatter created a cacophony that only added to the chaos of the situation.

As Troy was shoved out of the front doors, he spotted Jane's friends hurrying through a side door, unseen in the crowd. He breathed a sigh of relief: so far, the plan was on track.

Across the pavement, scientists gathered and stared up with varying expressions of confusion at the building. They were clearly wondering where the fire was.

The Plugs trudged further and further from the building, the guards' hands tight around their arms. It had been a few minutes now…Jordan and the rest of the combat fighters should be coming in guard uniforms any second. Like clockwork, they hurried around a corner of the facility, blending perfectly with the rest of security. Racing over to the Plugs, they pretended to sound panicked.

Jordan spoke. "They want you seven over there to round up the scientists. We've got these ingrates covered." He motioned impatiently to the Plugs. It seemed like time paused for a moment; like the wind had stopped moving and the air had compressed. The guards appeared to stop and think over their orders, and all the Plugs could do was pray that their plan would continue to work. Finally, the guards nodded hesitantly. They were convinced. Jordan and his allies gripped the Plugs' arms tightly and led Brice, Lydia, Jared, Troy, Antonia, and Emily around the back.

Jordan gave them a quick briefing. "Alright, Vicky and Gabe are inside right now. They're working on breaking into the system. But we've gotta hurry. The bombs are in place, and they're set to detonate in exactly twenty minutes. You guys should do what you've gotta do, and then get the hell out of here as soon as possible."

They nodded curtly and pushed through the heavy metal door, back into the facility.

Rushing up the stairs, the Plugs and the combat fighters scrambled to the lab where Vicky and Gabe sat hunched over the computers.

Vicky sounded exasperated when she finally spoke. "We've gotten through three layers of security, but we need one more password. Do any of you have an idea what it could be?!" She whipped her head around to face them, fingers still typing away on the computer.

Lydia began to think aloud. "Ummm…try all of our names. No, try the project's start date. Or…what about an abbreviation of sorts?"

Password after password was denied, and they were running out of time.

Mitch sat in the background; he had been brought in to help with passwords and security since he knew the most about the facilities. But now, he sat silent in the corner, a dark expression passing over his face.

Suddenly, he rose to his full height out of the darkness and pulled his hand out from underneath the folds of his shirt. He was aiming his gun at Vicky.

# CHAPTER FORTY-NINE

"Mitch, what the hell are you doing?" Lydia asked. "We don't have time for that. Do you know what the password could be? We really need your help on this one," she pleaded.

But Mitch took another step forward, and his gun clicked. Lifting his arm up, he pointed the barrel at Vicky's head.

"You six…come with me, or I'll shoot."

Now it was time for Emily to speak. "What are you talking about? We're on your side, Mitch! C'mon, you need to help us!"

He only started shaking in response. "I can't run around in circles anymore. I'm not a hero, Em. I've gotta do this…you gave me no choice." His voice shook with emotion.

"Please, please, just listen! I don't know what you mean. I promise, Mitch, we will take care of you! We'll be your family. We'll find you a place to live. Anywhere is better than here! I swear, it'll be a better life than you've ever known."

"If I've learned anything," he spat, "it's that you can't take risks in this world. There is no such thing as family. I never should've come with you. All I needed was to prove myself, and now I finally, finally have the chance. I'll save my mom's job. You can't hack into the system, she's too smart for you. She makes the passwords…I'll save the project. They'll absolutely worship me, Em. Do you understand that? They'll worship me. So please, just come with me. We can be happy, we can live together, and you'll never be alone again. I'll never be alone again. We can start a life together and you can produce energy and I can help study you and..." he lost himself in his thoughts. "Please."

The desperateness in his voice made Emily's heart break. What had happened to that sweet, shy kid she'd first met? Snapping back to reality, she saw him step closer to Vicky and grip her shoulder. Now, the gun was pressed against her head.

"One last chance," he pleaded.

The scene played out in front of her slowly, like time was melting away in slow motion. Mitch turned his head to Vicky. He moved both hands to the gun. And in a split second of confusion, in a split second of fear and panic and desperation, Emily whipped out her gun. She aimed. She shot.

It was his scream that brought her back to reality; his scream that confirmed what she'd just done. Falling to his side, Emily lifted his head onto her knees. "I'm so sorry," she gasped, horrified. Her hands turned crimson. All feeling fled from her body, and she realized how far she was from the girl in Duluth, the girl running on the treadmill and dreaming of her future. "I'm-I'm so sorry, Mitch. I just couldn't let you do it. I couldn't let you kill her." His face grew fuzzy through her tears, but she wiped them away hastily.

Mitch only blinked back in response and shifted his gaze to her eyes. He was shuddering violently, taking short little gasps that made his chest quiver. "I'm-I'm s-sorry, Em...I l-let it run in th-the blood, di-didn't I?"

Emily couldn't bear to watch the life fade from his eyes. She turned away, trying to hide her tears.

A sharp breath shuddered throughout his entire body; finally, Mitch went limp.

And then he was gone.

"No, no, Mitch, please, stay!" Emily screamed hysterically. "Stay! We'll figure all this out, I swear-I-I promise!" Emily shook him desperately, holding his limp hand, pretending she could still feel the faintest trace of a heartbeat somewhere in the fingertips. Remembering that first day they'd met, when he'd helped her escape the facility, she thought about where he'd come from. She realized that maybe he'd had it far worse than her; a forever bitter mother, a gone but not forgotten father, a—

But that was it. James, the never forgotten father. The same code Mitch had used to steal from Linda's safe. "James. James92349" she sputtered. "That's the password."

Vicky typed it in and hit enter. The ding of the password's approval rang out through the otherwise silent room.

# CHAPTER FIFTY

Emily clung to Mitch's lifeless body, her head resting against his chest. In her right hand, she still held the gun loosely. Her body heaved with sobs. When Lydia tried to pull her away, she only pushed back in anger. "Leave me alone! Leave! Go without me! I'll die with the bomb. I don't care anymore. I'm…I'm so sorry. I put you in danger. I thought…I thought I could trust him," Emily shook, wrapping her arms around herself and rocking back and forth in a dazed state. "I'm not myself, not anymore. Look what this has done to me," she motioned all around her. "Look what they've done to me," she shouted angrily, pointing outside to where the scientists had gathered. "I will not let them do this to one more person," she declared firmly.

"Please just come with us," Lydia pleaded.

"Emily, please. Come on. It's alright, now," Troy promised.

Not wanting to hold up her friends any longer, Emily took a final glance at Mitch. His scruffy hair now had droplets of blood in it, already drying and solidifying along with the scarring image locked into Emily's mind. She covered her face and allowed herself to be lead away by her friends.

The Plugs hurried out of the room, leaving Vicky and her team to make sure the entire system's database was completely wiped clean. There were only five minutes left until the bombs went off, and they raced out the back door and towards the woods behind the headquarters.

Troy skidded to a stop, glancing at the building. "What do we do now?!" he shouted over the noise. His voice broke.

Emily stared at her friends, face still wet with tears. "I think we know what needs to be done. Don't we?"

Lydia nodded. Jared sniffled, but bowed his head in agreement. Brice, Troy, and Antonia followed.

After seeing Mitch's betrayal, after seeing how this project had changed people and taken away their humanity, the decision was made for them. Although they'd avoided the topic at all costs, it was clear now what they had to do. Shouts enveloped the air around them as the Plugs ran further and further from the prison that had held them for so long. As they moved, they heard a huge explosion, and turned to watch the headquarters explode in a fiery ball of red. Despite the flames, the feeling of running felt so good to Lydia, and for a moment she felt ready; ready to leave this world behind and find a better one. Ready to watch the one she'd left behind change. And her heart practically burst with pride. They'd done it. They'd really done it.

The Plugs turned away from the building, forcing themselves to focus on the task at hand...they knew that there were no other options...no Plugs meant no information for the scientists to study, and they needed to make a statement, to make the project go public, bring media attention, so that all the trapped scientists could finally leave and no more children would suffer.

Stumbling away from the building, toppling infrastructure still shaking the ground, they headed for the tree line and slowed down. The Plugs had gone far enough, and they knew that if they waited any longer, they might lose their courage.

So many moments darted through their minds. Gratefulness that they had each other to make their lives worth living, no matter how short they were. A true love for one another, the type that burns deep within. The bond of family, the fact that this was all they had.

Voicing all of these emotions, Lydia decided to speak a final sentence. "No matter how short our lives were, we made the most of them with each other. And for that, I am forever grateful."

Everyone nodded. Their faces looked like they had aged years in just a few moments. One by one, they reached behind their back and found the small metal plug on their shoulders. Each of them took a deep breath and pulled, throwing them into a pile on the ground. Blood was already seeping through their shirts from the spots where the plugs had been. Pain shot down their arms and backs. On the ground, the blue-silver metal twitched, wires fizzling and twisting in on themselves, making them seem alive. They all looked up to Lydia, waiting for her to finish the job. Calmly, she reached into her pocket and pulled out a match. She'd told them that she would bring matches as backup, in case the bombs didn't work. Lydia took the final step, stooping to the ground and gently setting flame to all of the plugs to ensure they could never be reused or studied. They crackled and popped loudly as the fire enveloped them, and sparks shot upwards toward the sky and blended with the flames. Lydia watched patiently, dazedly, as the plugs made their final gasping noises and fizzled out. She stomped out the fire with her heel, grinding away all the research, all the science. With the sound of the fight still roaring in the background and the smoke still lingering in the air, the Plugs took one last glance at the world they so hoped would change. The flames surrounding the building finally began burning out, and the smoke swirled higher and higher into the air. The Plugs turned away from the final fight, their shirts now soaked with blood. And they sat down in their usual circle with joined hands, watching each other's faces and holding on more tightly than ever before.

# EPILOGUE

"Lydia!" Jane's voice boomed as she searched the area around the headquarters. The fire was almost gone now, only small bits of crumbling wall alight. The others had fled back to the apartment, but Jane stayed, searching for the Plugs. It was hard to tell whether they'd been taken or not, and the team's spirits were low. A fire truck stood alone on the street, the firefighter hosing down the last of the flames, while a newscaster posed in front of the building, camera men filming the ashes that remained of the headquarters.

During the fight, Jordan had run across some of the P.E.I. documents while placing bombs. Although the team had planned to destroy all of the scientists' findings, Jordan knew that they would need proof of the experiment to show to media outlets. It had been an unexpected find and an impulsive steal, but the papers held priceless information, outlining the details of the project and some of their most brutal tests. Even as Jane was searching for the Plugs, Angeline and Maria were organizing the paperwork and drafting letters to send to the most prominent news outlets.

Desperate, Jane scoured the tree line. As she bent to feel the hot ground, her fingers turning black, a crumpled sheet of paper fell from her pocket; Lydia's letter. Jane had almost forgotten all about it; she hadn't given the letter much thought when Lydia handed it to her and made her promise not to read it until after the battle. She picked up the paper quickly, smoothing it against the ground. Long, tight handwriting filled each line. Reading slowly, she struggled to comprehend each word; it was all a shock to her; an outcome she hadn't expected, an option she'd never imagined.

Jane—

I'm writing this shortly before we leave for the attack on headquarters, but I feel that it is necessary to make our actions worthwhile. I'm not sure if we'll be captured and taken back to our facilities, or if my predictions will come true. But supposing they do, I beg you to read this letter and read it closely.

What I need you to know is that if we don't return with you to the apartment, my friends and I have come to the decision to pull our plugs. If we make that decision, I'll lead them to the woods outside the headquarters. All I ask is that when you find us, you call the news stations. Make sure they take pictures immediately— I fear that the facilities will try to erase us from the world; they've controlled our lives, and I can't stand to let them control our deaths. You'll also need to submit my writings to the papers. I've hidden my lifelong journal and records in your kitchen cupboard; they'll tell you all I can remember about my experiences with the P.E.I. Please spread our story. Spread it and share what we've done, so that people might change. Then, this will all have been worth it.

Before I end this letter, I think I need to make something clear. I want you to know—I want everyone to know—that I never forced my idea of pulling our plugs upon my friends. Although I suspected that they might come to the same realization I'd come to since I left my facility in Arizona, it took them a bit longer to realize our only real option. I knew they soon would, but I could never mention the idea to them. I refuse to control my friends' lives like the P.E.I. did, because I understand now more than ever that lives aren't meant to be controlled. They're meant to be lived and spent and used, so that by the time we're done with them, they're cracked, worn in…loved. And that's at the heart of why we did all this. That's why we keep fighting for our freedom; because we have a right to live, and to live the way we want. If we believe in that, if we really know it and stand by it…no one can stop us. No one did.

Sincerely,
Lydia

# ABOUT THE AUTHOR

Tatum Samson lives in a small town in Massachusetts with her mom, her dad, and her older sister Faith. She also lives with her two furry friends, Dobby and Muggle. Tatum has always had an immense love for both reading and writing, and she is excited to release *Plugs* as her debut novel. In the future, she hopes to compose pieces in many different genres. Tatum's favorite types of books to read are science fiction, fantasy, and realistic fiction. She plans to continue writing novels, short stories, and poetry. To read more of Tatum's work or learn about upcoming projects and events, please visit:

Instagram: @tatumsamson
Twitter: @tatumsamson
Facebook: Tatum J Samson
Snapchat: tatumsamson
Website: tatumsamson.com

Made in the USA
Columbia, SC
21 May 2018